THE NAMING OF
William
Rutherford

For my children: Guy, Oliver and Thomas.

With thanks to the many people who
helped me during the writing of this
book. Special thanks are due to my
husband, Andy, to my friends at
Higham, and to John Clifford of Eyam.

THE NAMING OF
William
Rutherford

LINDA KEMPTON

MAMMOTH

First published in Great Britain 1992
by William Heinemann Ltd
Published 1994 by Mammoth
an imprint of Reed Consumer Books Ltd
Michelin House, 81 Fulham Road, London SW3 6RB
and Auckland, Melbourne, Singapore and Toronto

ISBN 0 7497 1581 2

A CIP catalogue record for this title
is available from the British Library

Printed in Great Britain
by Cox & Wyman Ltd, Reading, Berkshire

Chapter 1
The Nightmare

"Jack! Please help us! Please help us, Jack."

The little cradle creaked on curved rockers, creak, creak, on the flagstone floor; a tiny crib of dark brown wood, with carved acorns on each of the corners of the square wooden hood. Figures in long dresses and white bonnets surrounded it. One of them turned her face to Jack, an old face etched with lines. And down the lines ran tears. The mouth moved but there was no sound. The face pleaded with Jack, but he didn't know why.

A fire burned in a huge old fireplace made of stone. It was night. Candles flickered on the old-fashioned dresser. Candles that gave off thick, foul-smelling smoke and made monstrous shadows loom and dance on the grey stone walls.

The bodies came towards him. Huge faces peered into his and he could feel hot breath and smell woollen dresses, damp with sweat. The women dragged him towards the cot and pointed to a young child. Its hair was wet. Tiny globules of sweat patterned its fevered face. A young girl ran to him and took hold of his shoulders; looked into his face.

Jack tried to run but his legs refused. The heat oppressed him so that his body felt fixed like welded metal to the ground. There was no sound save the creaking of the cradle. Mouths and bodies moved. Faces and arms reached out to him, imploringly. Sound returned.

"Jack! Please help us!"

The cries rang around his head. Bodies pressed in on him so that he could hardly breathe. A deep rhythm of chanting voices echoed in his ears. And above the rhythm there pierced a shriller voice; a boy screaming.

"No! No! Let me out!"

Jack threshed and fought the smothering folds of clothes.

"Let go of me! Let me go!"

He gave a final wrench, but it was too hard. He fell into a stomach-turning blackness which seemed to go on for ever, but ended, at last, with a sudden thud. Onto the bedroom floor.

"No, don't, please don't."

The bedroom flooded with light and a single murmuring voice bore in on him again.

"Don't what, Jack? It's all right. It's me.

Mum."

"What?" Jack's eyes were screwed up against the light as his brain tried to sort out the muddled messages. Gradually, the fog of confusion began to clear.

"You've been dreaming. It's all right now."

A dream? Yes of course, that's all it was; a dream.

Jack climbed back into bed and huddled into the warmth of his duvet.

"Want to tell me about it?"

"No."

"In the morning then." Jack's mother smoothed his red hair.

"Goodnight."

"Goodnight. Mum?"

"Yes?"

"Don't turn the light out."

Jack hugged his knees to his chest and tried to shut out the ghostly images which danced around his brain. The thought of the dark was terrifying and the atmosphere of the dream refused to leave him.

It was still there in the morning after an almost sleepless night. At school, the day went from bad to worse.

"I suggest you stop daydreaming and start writing, Jack Rutherford."

Mr Nixon's quiet voice, just two inches from Jack's ear, made him turn quickly. His history book landed on the floor with a smack.

"What's the matter with you today?"

"Sorry."

"Well, get a move on. I'd have thought the Spanish Armada was right up your street."

Jack looked down at his book. Out of the corner of his eye he could see Tom grinning at him. Tom had written half a page.

At lunchtime the dining room was busy with conversation and the clatter of knives and forks. Jack tried to tell Tom about the dream.

"And there was this baby in an old-fashioned cradle."

Tom's mouth was full of ham and tomato sandwich. He grunted.

"It was dead scary."

"Oh no, yoghurt again. Swap it for your cake?"

"If you like." Jack wasn't hungry.

He spent the afternoon trying to keep awake. At break he leaned against the changing room wall and watched Tom playing football with two other boys. He didn't feel like joining in.

"You know what I think?" Tom was walking towards him, breathless and red in the face.

"No." Jack's voice was flat. At the moment he didn't care what Tom thought.

"I think you're going to catch some horrible disease. You look yucky."

"Thanks." He tried to smile but couldn't.

4

"Anyway, my mum says you're bound to be a bit upset."

"What about?"

"Having a new baby in the family."

"I am not upset."

"After being the only one for all these years."

"Look, it's not even born yet." He kicked at a stone angrily. How dare they talk about him behind his back! How dare they!

The antique shop was one of Jack's favourite places and he found himself, as always, wandering towards it.

It was a jumbly shop, just a small room, dark with dim corners which seemed to disappear into nothingness. Everything in the shop was crammed together. There were boxes full of books and plates and candlesticks. Stuffed animals in glass cases fell over photograph albums, tea sets and clocks. And if he was really lucky, there might be an old gas mask, or war medals.

Jack had almost passed the shop when he saw it. His heart seemed to stop beating. He swivelled round on his heels and stared. His breath caught in his throat.

The cradle stood behind a case of butterflies.

In two strides Jack was at the window, his forehead resting on the cold glass. His breath steamed it up, so that he had to rub it clear again. It was the same crib. The one in his dream. And it had not been in the shop yesterday. He was sure of it.

Jack gazed at the acorns on the corners of the hood, and at the date etched along the top, 1664. He knew that he had to have it. Knew more than that. Knew that he was meant to have it. The dream reached out from the depths of the crib, seeming to draw him into it.

It was not easy to turn away. But as he did so, Jack noticed a price tag, hanging from one of the acorns. He tilted his head almost upside down so that he could read it, and then whistled softly to himself. It was very expensive.

He dug his hands deeply into his pockets and began to walk home. Past the butcher's shop with its blue tiles and cold floor, the flower shop with its red and white striped awning, and the newsagent's where two or three newspapers still hung on the rack outside. The High Street was busy with traffic. Thick fumes filled the darkening air.

The argument going on in Jack's head was like a ping-pong game. I really want this cradle! But why? What would my friends think? Yesterday I wanted a mountain bike more than anything in the world. Now I want a cradle. It's not normal. What would Tom say? Not that I'd tell him. He'd think I was mad. But the cradle wants me too. Don't be daft. You're cracking up. Boys of your age don't want cradles. Best forget about it.

But by the time Jack reached home, he knew that he could not forget it. It would not let him.

Leaving the gate open as usual, he walked up the path that skirted the house to the right. He would talk to his mother at tea-time.

Jack sagged in his chair like an old beanbag and glared at his mother from behind his glasses.

"It's no good looking at me like that. I don't want an antique cradle. I want a new one. And what have you done to your glasses again?"

Jack sighed. "I fell over." Best not to say anything about his encounter with Simon Smith.

He took his glasses off and looked at them glumly. He'd stuck the earpiece to the lens with sticking plaster, but it hadn't worked. The earpiece was nearly off again.

"Well, if it happens once more you'll have to pay for them to be mended."

"Yes." Jack gave another sigh.

There was silence in the kitchen apart from the sound of plates being stacked.

"Anyway, I've seen a lovely cot in Babyjoy."

Babyjoy! Jack raised his eyebrows in disgust. It'd probably have pink rabbits on it.

There was a blob of gravy on the tablecloth.

7

He worked it round and round with his finger until it wouldn't spread any further.

"Mum?"

"What?"

"Go and have a look at this one first. Please."

"If it's as old as you say, it'll be very expensive."

"What about that posh pram you're going to buy? Couldn't you get a cheaper one?"

"No, I've set my heart on that one."

"Well, I just hope none of my friends see you pushing it around, that's all. It looks like something out of a museum with those great big wheels."

"I expect the cradle looks like something out of a museum too, doesn't it?"

"Yes, but that's different. You wouldn't be pushing it around the streets would you?"

His mother banged the plates back into the old pine dresser.

"Mum, you have to pass the antique shop to get to the supermarket. Just look in the window. You can't miss it." He put his glasses back on. They slanted across his face at an alarming angle.

"Anyway, since when have you been interested in cradles?"

Jack shrugged. Since the dream, that's when. But he wasn't going to tell her that; she'd think he'd gone loopy. Come to think of it, perhaps he had.

Mum stood beside him, her hands folded on the bump where his brother or sister lived.

"I'll have a look, but that's all I'm doing. Don't raise your hopes."

He said nothing. The grin on his face said it all.

"Thanks, Mum."

"I don't know what you're thanking me for."

"Because when you see the cradle you'll love it."

His mother grunted and pulled the tablecloth from under her son's arms. He stood up silently, knocking his chair against the radiator so that it made a curious zinging noise.

"I'm going to see Tom."

"What's the rush?"

But he was already halfway up the stairs and travelling fast. There was no reply.

It was tea-time on the following day. Mum had a dreamy look on her face which her son recognised. He could never quite get through to her when she looked like this.

"Hey, Mum." Jack spoke softly. He waved a hand in front of her as if trying to wake her from a trance.

"Is there anybody there?"

She laughed. "Sorry. I was miles away."

"Where? Where were you?"

His mother dropped three teabags into the teapot and poured on the boiling water. She was pretending not to hear. It was something she did when she didn't want to talk.

"Where were you, Mum?"

She laughed again. "Oh, nowhere very important."

"Leave your mother alone, there's a good lad. She's tired."

The voice came from behind a very large newspaper. The only sign that anyone was there, was two sets of fingers at either side. His father was always buying, reading, or discussing newspapers. Jack couldn't understand it. Newspapers always looked so boring.

"Food, Duncan." Mum pushed the plate as near as possible to Dad's place without getting the newspaper in it.

"Ah, food."

Yes, food, thought Jack. His father had a habit of echoing everything that was said to him.

I wonder if that's how he goes on in the surgery? I can just imagine it?:

I've got a sore knee, Dr Rutherford.

A sore knee?

Yes, a sore knee.

Ah, a sore knee.

Jack was grinning at the thought of this little

pantomime when he realised that his mother was talking to him.

"I said would you like more bacon?"

"Yes, please." Jack never refused more bacon. He wondered why his mother bothered to ask.

"Why are you tired?"

"What?"

"Dad said you were tired."

"Because she's having a baby," said Dad, as he upended a bottle of brown sauce all over his bacon.

Ask a silly question!

"And because she's spent all day looking at cots."

"Cots?" Jack's heart thudded in his chest.

He looked up to see his mother giving his father the sort of glance which means, You shouldn't have said that.

"Did you see the cradle in the antique shop?" He was surprised at how calm his voice sounded. As though the answer were of no particular interest to him.

"Yes, I did."

"And?"

The silence was like the air before a thunderstorm. His mother was looking at her plate and chasing a piece of bacon around with her fork.

"You were right, Jack. I love it."

Dad picked up his paper and pushed his chair back from the table. "And it's too expensive, so don't go hatching any plots behind my back."

Nobody said anything.

"I've got surgery in five minutes and I'm going to be late." He always said this, even though the surgery was attached to the house and he had only to go through a door to get there.

Mother and son sat in silence. The kitchen clock ticked.

"Why don't you go and buy the cradle, Mum?" said Jack, at last. "You go to work too. It's not only Dad who earns the money, is it?"

"No. No, it isn't."

"You're a doctor, the same as him. It's not fair that he should make all the decisions."

"It's not like that, Jack. He doesn't make all the decisions. We talk things over. It's just that we can't agree about this."

"Well, you and me agree, so it's two against one. We win."

His mother laughed.

"Mum? Did you feel anything when you saw the cradle?" As soon as he'd spoken, Jack wished he could have picked the words out of the air and put them away again. He hadn't meant to say anything. He hadn't told his mother about the dream, even when she'd asked.

"What d'you mean?" His mother looked at him with her head on one side and a slight frown on her forehead. There was no going back now.

"It's just that I've got this feeling that we're supposed to have it. That it's meant to belong to us somehow." Jack looked down at the table. He felt stupid now he'd said it out loud.

His mother's voice was low, and she had that dreamy look on her face again.

"That's just how I felt."

Jack looked at her. And knew that she understood.

Chapter 2
Snowstorm

Only another half an hour to go before the end of school. Thank Goodness! thought Jack. He gazed out of the window, watching the curious change of light in the afternoon sky. A computer hummed, unheeded, in front of him.

"It's going to snow," said Tom.

The two boys sat in an alcove just outside the classroom door. They both loved computers and were working on an English project together. But Jack was bored today. He wanted to be alone so that he could think.

"I said it's going to snow. Look."

"I am looking." The clouds had been lowering all afternoon, silently, ominously, like an army preparing for battle. Now they had stopped. It was still and silent. The calm before the storm. Inside the classroom, twenty-six heads watched, hardly breathing. And then the first flakes fell.

14

"It's snowing!" The spell was broken. Noise and clamour erupted. Excitement took hold and spread. Jack poked his head round the door, wanting to join in.

"All right. You've all seen snow before. Calm down."

Shouts subsided to murmurs.

"Quiet!"

The murmurs stopped.

"Right. Put your things away and we'll have another chapter of our story."

There were cries of, "Great!" "Brilliant!" "Fantastic!"

Jack called to Tom to switch off the computers, then found his place in the middle of the restless, shuffling class.

"There's only two more pages to the end of the chapter," said Mr Nixon. "Close your eyes and try to concentrate."

The bell rang as Mr Nixon closed the book.

The cheers were deafening. Desk lids banged, feet scuffled, voices clamoured. Mr Nixon rubbed his hands together and said nothing.

"Bye, Sir."

"Bye, Mr Nixon."

"Bye, Sir. Can we have the day off tomorrow?"

"Yes, Sir. It'll be too bad to get to school."

"Bet there'll be no heating tomorrow, Sir."

"The power lines'll be down."

Mr Nixon smiled. "Good afternoon, everyone."

Jack and Tom charged from the school building with hordes of other children, in a scramble of bodies, coats, hats and scarves. Already the first snowballs had been thrown. Shouting voices pierced the air.

Outside the school gates, Jack's hand travelled along the top of a hedge, gathering snow.

The two boys slipped and slid towards home, making plans to go sledging. As they approached the shops a barrage of snowballs came hurling through the air. One caught Jack on the side of his face.

"Who the heck's that?" He brushed the snow from his face.

"It's Simon Smith. Look." Tom pointed.

Jack was just in time to see a couple of grinning faces disappearing behind a low wall.

"Quick! This way," Tom hissed. They ran along the front of the shops and veered off down a narrow alleyway which split the row of buildings in half. It was dark and slippery but it brought them out behind their attackers. They could creep up on them, unnoticed.

They emerged from the alleyway, slowed down, and started to edge towards the other two boys. Jack's heart was pounding, every sense alert.

"Let's stop here," whispered Tom. "Then we can get a good stock of ammunition ready."

"Yeah. Then we'll let 'em have it." Jack grinned. His glasses were smeared with melting snow and he could hardly see. He took them off and wiped them with the dry end of his scarf. They were covered with tiny fibres of red wool, but they'd have to do.

"I need windscreen wipers," he complained.

"What? Oh, yes." Tom was busy piling up his supplies. "Come on, Jack. Never mind your glasses."

"Well, I'm not going to be much good if I can't see where I'm throwing, am I?" He peeped cautiously round the corner. "I can't see them."

"What?"

"They've gone."

"Come here, four eyes. Let me have a look."

There was a woman with a shopping basket and another walking a dog. No sign of the boys.

"Oh, no. Now they'll think we were scared." Tom sat on his heels and scratched his head through his thick, blond hair.

Before Jack could reply, a fury of bodies flew at the two boys, throwing them to the ground.

Jack lay face down in the snow, winded by the force of the attack. He felt a snowball, excruciatingly cold, forced down his back, and the push of bony fingers on his warm skin. He tried to move, but a hand pinned his neck to the ground. The owner of the hand sat on him.

"Your ears are dirty, Jack. Tut-tut, what would your Mummy say? And her a doctor too. I'm going to have to wash them out for you." Simon Smith picked up a pile of snow with his free hand, and slapped it into Jack's ear. He pushed it in until Jack felt as though his eardrum was going to burst.

"Get off, you pig! You just wait!"

Panting and struggling, Jack finally managed to throw him off his back. Simon rolled over. Jack worked quickly. He scooped up an enormous mound of snow and threw it into Simon's unprotected face. He retrieved his glasses which had come off during the struggle and put them in his pocket. They might be safer there.

Jack pushed the other boy off Tom. David Clarke; he might have known. But Simon Smith was back on his feet again. He threw himself at Jack and they both came down in the snow. The other two joined in and there was an indiscriminate flurry of arms and legs. In the end, no-one was sure who they were fighting.

"Truce!" yelled Tom.

"Yeah, truce," agreed David Clarke.

The four bodies separated and lay panting on

the ground. Jack was on his back with his mouth open, catching the snowflakes which were still whirling furiously through the dark. His hands and face burned with cold and there was a deep ache in his right ear.

"Better be getting home," said Tom, ever practical. He sat up slowly and groaned.

"Good idea." Jack closed his mouth on his last helping of snowflakes and stood up. He held out his hand to Simon Smith.

"Quits, Simon?"

Simon ignored it. "For the time being."

The four boys had split up and Jack was walking past the shops alone. He had given Simon Smith a dose of his own medicine and he was pleased with himself.

As he approached the antique shop, it occurred to him that he hadn't thought about the cradle for almost an hour. Perhaps his obsession was over. He came within sight of the window and knew that it was not. The cradle had gone. The shock knocked the breath from his body like one of Simon Smith's punches.

Jack felt for his glasses and put them on. But they made no difference. The crib had definitely gone. Someone must have bought it.

Jack trudged home, all pleasure gone, his triumph forgotten. Somebody else had bought the cradle. And he was meant to have it, not them.

At the back door, he had to stop himself from running in and crying all over his mother. He swallowed hard and clenched his jaw. He spoke sternly to himself. I am not going to cry. I am not. He pushed open the door.

"Hello, Jack. Snow thick enough for you?"

His mother was beating eggs. She was smiling. She wouldn't be smiling for long. Not when he told her.

He swallowed twice and looked at the eggs, pale yellow, topped with a mass of tiny bubbles. Ridiculously, he heard the cookery teacher's voice in his head: "Beating incorporates air into the mixture." He burst into tears.

It was a long time before he could say anything. He felt a fool. His mother had both her arms round him, but the bump got in the way. For some reason, he felt angry with it.

"The cradle's gone." The room was filled with the enormity of his statement, as though saying it had made the cradle's disappearance more real.

"Yes, I know."

"What? How d'you know?"

"Come upstairs. " She took Jack by the hand as though he were a four year old. But he didn't mind. Through the hall, up the stairs, and into the baby's room.

The cradle stood in the corner. It had come home.

"And that's final!" A door slammed upstairs and Dr Rutherford's heavy footsteps thudded across the landing.

Jack sat at the kitchen table with his fingers in his ears and his eyes screwed up. But this wasn't enough to block out the row going on upstairs. He didn't take too much notice of his father's tempers as a rule; they were a bit like fireworks: loud, colourful and brief. But this was an important row.

Finally, although it was painful, Jack couldn't bear not to know what was going on. He went to the bottom of the stairs and sat down.

"Have you any idea how much that cradle cost?"

"Of course I have, d'you think I'm stupid? I bought it." His mother's voice was lower than his father's, but much clearer. "The money's in the bank, earmarked for baby equipment. In any case, it's money that I've worked for. And I shall be working again in a few month's time. Don't forget that!"

And so it went on, and on, until the telephone rang.

"I've got to see a patient."

Jack moved hurriedly from the bottom of the stairs, as his father came down.

"And Pauline."

"What?"

"That cradle's going back in the morning. I'll take it myself." He slammed the door before his wife could reply.

As soon as the catch clicked, Jack ran up the stairs, two at a time. His mother was on the landing kicking the clothes-basket.

"Mum, you're not going to let him take it back, are you?"

She picked up the basket with a heavy sigh. "I don't know, Jack."

"Mum!"

"It was a lot of money to spend without talking it over first, I suppose. I'd be annoyed if he'd done the same thing to me."

Jack looked at his mother with his mouth open and his eyes wide. He couldn't believe it. "Why do you always stick up for him?"

"Because he's worth sticking up for. And don't talk about your father like that."

"Like what?" Honestly! Jack didn't understand his parents at times. You'd think they couldn't bear each other sometimes, the way they shouted. But just try and criticise one of them and you were in big trouble.

"Time for bed, Jack."

It would be!

It was midnight and Jack hadn't slept. He couldn't find a comfortable position, and the pillows were lumpy. The row was replaying itself in his head, like a cassette on automatic rewind. He couldn't lie there any longer. His brain was racing and he felt so full of energy that he could have run a mile.

Jack crept along the landing to the baby's room. He opened the door gently, pushed cautiously. The door squeaked. There was a cough from his parents' room and the sound of creaking springs, as one of them turned over in their ancient bed.

His father had left the garden light on. There was a soft pool of yellow light in the little bedroom.

The cradle welcomed him.

He bent down and set it rocking gently, remembering the dream. Now that the cradle was here, he was no longer afraid. He ran his fingers over the date, 1664. Someone had made this cradle more than three hundred years ago. Over three hundred years had passed since the first baby had slept in it. Jack was filled with a deep contentment.

Through the low window, he could see the snow still falling, piling high, flake upon flake. He could see the outline of the three huge oaks standing side by side, their branches spread widely, almost touching one another. They drooped slightly with the weight of the snow. The old, delapidated summerhouse was covered, and there was no distinction between the lawn, the path and the borders. The garden was a white blanket, unbroken by lines. It was difficult to see much beyond the summerhouse. The snow was falling so densely that everything beyond it was blurred and indistinct.

Jack watched the snowflakes fall through the yellow light. The little room seemed to glow in the quietness of the house and the stillness of the night. Snow had muffled sound. Only snowflakes moved.

He touched the cradle again. His fingers found one of the curved acorns. It was loose. As he turned it, he felt dizzy. His head began to spin. With each turn of the acorn it span faster and faster. He couldn't stop. His whole body churned and toppled. He swayed and felt himself falling. Falling through space and darkness, on and on, as though he would never stop. Cold fingers stroked his face. Icy whispers breathed his name. "Jack, Jack, Jack."

Chapter 3
The Strange Village

The falling sensation stopped and Jack was jolted onto a wooden floor. A baby cried and something hit Jack on the shoulder: bang, stop, bang, stop, bang, stop. It was the cradle. A girl's voice shouted in alarm.

Jack lay on his back and blinked up at the inside of a thatched roof. Someone rushed past him and snatched at the wailing infant. "Hush, William; hush."

The girl looked just as she had in the dream. The same wisps of blond hair straggled from under a white bonnet; the same brown dress reached to the floor. She hugged the baby close. Jack sat up.

"Mother! Mother!" The girl opened a door and ran out, screaming.

Jack shook his head and looked around the room. Sunlight filtered through a small window and specks of dust floated in its beam.

His mouth was dry and he tried to swallow.

He could hear footsteps climbing stairs; getting nearer. Jack dived under a little bed in the corner, but it was too low. The door opened as he was trying to get his bottom half to follow the top.

"Where is he?" A woman's voice.

Jack felt faint. The room was stuffy and his backside still protruded. Only one thing for it; he wriggled backwards until he was out.

"There, Mother!" The girl screamed again. "Can you not see him?"

"No madam, I can not." She put the baby back in the cradle and turned to her daughter again.

"He is there!" The girl pointed at Jack and began to cry softly.

The woman followed her daughter's pointing finger and looked at Jack, her lined face full of fear. But then she looked away again as though she hadn't seen him.

"There is nought to see, child." She picked at the hem of her apron and said, in an angry whisper. "Tell no one of this apparition, else you are taken for a witch."

The girl gasped and cried louder; the baby joined in; Jack stood up.

"Mother." Her voice was a trembling whisper. She looked at Jack with eyes stretched in fear.

The woman slapped at her daughter's arm.

"I will not hear such nonsense, Susannah!" She put her hand to her head and said, in a quieter voice that verged on tears, "I pray to God that you are not possessed."

"Mother, I am not! I am not possessed!"

"Seek the Lord's guidance in prayer, that He may take these fancies from you."

The woman picked up the baby again and went out. Jack's knees shook and there was a crawling feeling in his stomach. He watched the girl in her old-fashioned clothes, edging towards the door.

"I didn't mean to scare you," he said.

At the sound of Jack's voice the girl's head snapped upwards; her fists flew to her mouth and then, slowly, she lowered them to her chin. She closed her eyes and mumbled something under her breath. Jack could see her lips moving, as if she were praying.

Her eyes opened slowly as though checking to see if he was still there or not. When she saw that he was, she spoke to him in a small, fearful voice.

"How came you here, apparition?"

"You're the apparition, not me," protested Jack.

Fresh tears welled in the girl's eyes. "No, I'm not; I'm not indeed." She spoke quietly and firmly, almost to herself, "Nor a witch; nor possessed."

She lifted her apron and covered her face with it, her fists clenching and unclenching all the while. Her shoulders lifted gently, and Jack heard the sound of quiet sobs.

"There's nothing to be scared of." Jack wished his words sounded more convincing. A grown woman couldn't see him apparently; that was scary.

The girl shrieked as Jack moved towards her. She clutched at the edge of the door more tightly and her breath came in shudders.

"Lord deliver me from this apparition. Lord deliver me." The girl sank to her knees, deeply sobbing.

Jack drew away. He'd never seen anyone behave like this before. It was weird. He wasn't anybody's idea of a hunky hero like Tom; that had to be faced; but people didn't usually react to him as badly as this.

He told himself that it wasn't his fault; that he hadn't asked to come here; that it wasn't as if he'd barged in through the front door without knocking. He shook his head. It was weird; really, really weird.

And he hadn't the remotest idea of what he ought to do. It would help if he knew where he was. One thing was for sure though: however he had come to be in this place, he had not travelled alone; the cradle had come with him.

It was his cradle, yet curiously changed. All the small marks and scratches, the signs of age, had disappeared. It seemed newer somehow.

He looked round the bare room with its stone walls and wide floorboards. He looked up into the sloping roof again and wondered why there was no ceiling. He turned and caught the girl watching him. She looked away.

Jack pretended to be interested in a sampler lying on the bed. A tiny green and blue house had been worked in cross-stitch, and underneath this, the words:

Except the Lord build the house,
They labour in vain that build it.

There was a name at the bottom, and a date: Susannah Roe, 1660. She must have been a great grandmother or something, to this Susannah, thought Jack, and started counting on his fingers. 1660, that would make her a great-great-great-great-great . . .

"How came you here, boy?"

Jack turned, startled from his arithmetic.

So, she was willing to admit that he was a boy and not an apparition, was she? Progress indeed! He drew a deep breath; and started to explain. It helped him to talk about it, and besides, the girl ought to be made to see that none of this was his fault.

But she could not, or would not, understand. "No. No. That can not be," she said.

It can not be. She's right, he thought; it can not be.

His head felt like an empty space where isolated thoughts darted around, looking for other thoughts. He would have to wait for them to find each other. Then he'd understand.

"Where am I?" His voice sounded too loud in this quiet place.

The girl had edged round the door and was almost out of the room. She took a step backwards and looked at Jack.

"You are in Eyam, boy. Are you a simpleton that you do not know where your two good legs have brought you?"

"I told you; it's not my two good legs that got me here."

There was no reply. Jack heard footsteps on the stairs. The girl had gone.

"I'd like to go home now." His words fell into the empty room, unheeded. "I'd like to go home now." He was shouting this time; his voice an assault on the quiet stillness. Only the silence answered.

Fear began to prick at his spine; to clutch at his chest. He ran to the door and flung it open. He must find a telephone; phone Mum. Let her know he was all right. Ask her to pick him up.

He ran down the steep, uneven stairs, into a kitchen; the kitchen of his dream. Fear, like a moving hand, rose into his throat and threatened to strangle him. He could hear his breath, rasping like an old man's. He felt dizzy.

The girl and her mother loomed towards him; towered over him. Then they pulled back, shrinking into the corner of the room. Then back towards him again, growing bigger; the figures looming and shrinking, looming and shrinking like the grotesque shapes in a hall of mirrors. The chanting voices of his dream came back to him; heat wrapped around him, stifled him. Heat, voices, faces, heat, voices, faces, heat, voices, faces.

"No!"

But the faces and voices chased him, came after him as he ran through the rectangle of light that blazed beyond the open door: ran into a lane that quietly absorbed the beatings of a merciless sun. There was space here, there was air. He could breathe.

Jack bent forward, his hands on his knees. The sun pierced needles of fire into his back. The rasping in his throat subsided. He took deep, deliberate breaths, willing himself to calm down.

And then a voice whispered his name, "Jack." Fear ebbed away and left behind it a space in his mind, an area of stillness which was outside of time. It was a special place, a place of light and knowledge that lay hidden behind a door with no handle. He reached out to it but the door was closing, closing.

Jack straightened up and looked around him at a village street. At least he thought it was a village: it was small and old and had thatched roofs. Stone cottages curved uphill and the narrow lane was just a rubble of earth and stones, ridged and pitted like a farm track. The smell of the place was overpowering: sewage and hay, smoke and food, all mixed together and strengthened in the heat of the sun, as though the smells had been cooked. Eyam, that's what the girl had said; Eyam.

The girl was peeping from behind the cottage door. She pulled back quickly as Jack came in. The baby was toddling round the floor and the mother was emptying hot fat into a bowl full of dripping. Jack cleared his throat.

"Look, I'm sorry to have barged in on you like this, but can you tell me how to get home? Is there a telephone I can use?"

The mother carried on as if he hadn't spoken. The girl looked away and said nothing.

"I've said I'm sorry. If you'll just tell me where I can find a telephone."

As Jack spoke, he knew that there was no

telephone. Not here; not in the whole village. It was as if two of his isolated thoughts had suddenly collided. There was no point in asking.

"Susannah, it is high time the water was fetched. Be sharp."

"Yes, Mother."

The girl picked up two wooden buckets from the side of the open fireplace.

"I'll come with you." Jack followed the girl into the street. "I may as well," he said conversationally, "There's nothing else to do."

"Go away," the girl hissed at him.

"I would if I could. How far's Derby?"

"Derby? Oh, Derby is many miles from here. 'Tis the other end of the earth I shouldn't wonder."

She turned away from Jack and walked more quickly, clanking the buckets backwards and forwards.

"What's wrong?"

No answer.

"What's wrong?"

She bit her lip, half-looked at Jack, slid her eyes to the ground.

"How can I speak to you if you are not there? You are but proof of the sin in me, and I almost forgot it."

"But I am there. Here, I mean. Course I'm here. Where else would I be?"

Well, I've been accused of some things in my time, thought Jack; but never of not being there. Maybe I *don't* really exist. Maybe I've just imagined myself. If I stop imagining, perhaps I'll disappear.

His musings were interrupted by a child's voice. The little boy was holding a woman's hand and they were coming closer. Their strange dress reminded Jack of a film he had seen once about a place in America. The people had been Amish, a bit like Quakers, and they'd cut themselves off from the outside world. They had no cars or modern machinery and dressed in old-fashioned clothes. It suddenly occurred to him that Eyam might be the English equivalent. That's it! Mystery solved. He felt pleased with himself for the way he'd worked things out. Take a bow, Jack Rutherford.

"Good day, Mistress Buckley; Isaac."

"Good day, Susannah."

Go on then, ignore me. Jack folded his arms, angrily. Only the girl seemed able to see him; and she refused to believe her own eyes. This place might seem like Amish country, thought Jack, but it doesn't explain how I came here, or why people can't see me.

They had arrived at two stone troughs filled with water. A woman was bending over one of them, washing clothes. Jack felt like tugging at her shoulder and saying, Look, it's me, Jack Rutherford from Derby. Say hello to me. But he didn't. He said, "If people tell you you're not real, then after a while you start to believe it."

The girl looked at the washerwoman nervously, but she carried on rubbing and wringing.

"Go away!"

"It's amazing how much anger can be conveyed in a whisper," said Jack, pompously.

She turned her back on him and plunged the buckets into the other trough. She pulled them out slowly, battling with the weight of the water. The earth around the troughs was thick and muddy, imprinted with footmarks. The girl squelched through it without seeming to notice. But then, thought Jack, someone as dirty as her wouldn't mind that sort of thing. He put one trainer lightly onto the mud. When he removed it, he saw his own footprint, perfectly outlined.

"There you are, you see! Ghosts don't leave footprints!" He tugged at the girl's arm with one hand and pointed to the footprint with the other, feeling all the triumph of someone who has been proved right.

The girl put down her buckets and looked suspiciously at the muddy print. Jack made another one, to prove the point.

"It signifies nothing," she said, and picked

up the buckets again.

There's just no telling some people, thought Jack. She doesn't want to believe in me, so she's not going to: end of discussion. Perhaps she'll change her mind if she sees how nice I am.

"Shall I carry one?" Jack held out his hand for a bucket.

The girl pulled away from him. "I do not need the help of demons."

"I am not a demon," said Jack, indignantly. "I am lost in this dirty, smelly village of yours, without so much as a telephone. And you've got no manners."

"And you speak strangely. Teler what? What witchcraft is it? I never heard such a word before."

The girl walked more quickly, trying to get rid of him.

Jack hurried to keep up with her. She was the only one who could see him and therefore the only one who could help. She might not be much use, but she was all he'd got.

"How am I going to get back?"

The girl stopped and banged her buckets onto the ground, so that water slopped over the side of them. She looked straight at him.

"Why have you chosen to torment me? Are there not people more wicked than Susannah Roe? What do you want from me?"

The fact that she didn't believe in him had been amusing at first, then slightly irritating. Now he was stunned by her fear and resentment. It was hard to believe that good, old, boring Jack Rutherford was the cause of such feelings.

"I just want to go home, that's all." His voice limped, as though he'd injured it.

"Well, boy, if you got here by turning a knob on the cot, as you say, then surely you can return that way." She stared at him as though willing him to go, as though she believed the force of her will might make it happen.

The simple sense of this suggestion filled Jack with a sudden hopeful energy. It seemed such an obvious solution.

"Thanks; you could be right."

He bounced down the lane as if he had springs on his feet. He was followed by Susannah and a clanking of buckets.

The woman sat at the kitchen table peeling vegetables, with the baby on her knee. The knife flashed in the sunlight and the baby tried to grab hold of it.

"Susanah, take hold of your brother before he cuts himself. And wipe your face, girl. Running in such heat."

The little boy lifted his short arms and shrieked happily. His sister picked him up and cuddled him, his legs astride her hips. He wore a long dress like a shepherd's smock which had wriggled up to reveal a damp nappy, tied in a knot at his waist. A white cap covered his hair.

For a second, none of the family moved or spoke. They seemed fixed, like a video with the pause button on. Then William chuckled. Jack ran upstairs.

He turned the acorn quickly; prayed to get back again. Please God, don't let me be stuck here. Please. I'll do anything, just let me get back. Then blackness surrounded him and his head swam in a pool of churning waves.

A voice sobbed in the darkness.

"Jack. Wake up."

His mother shook his shoulder, gently. Her voice and touch penetrated the dark. He was cold.

"Jack. Into bed with you, love." She steered him by the shoulders. He could feel soft carpet under his feet, hear the loud tick of the grandfather clock in the hall, see the dark-softened outline of his bed. Then he was awake; wide awake.

Was it a dream? It couldn't have been. He'd been able to smell and touch and feel. And what a funny name: Eyam. He looked into the darkness, strained to remember every detail. At last though, his thoughts settled to more gentle rhythms. He slept.

It was still dark when he woke next morning. He got out of bed and dressed, comforted by the smell of toast drifting up from the kitchen. He could hear the sounds of early morning: kettle and teapot, cups and saucers.

He opened the kitchen door and heard his mother's voice, " . . . and he was fast asleep by the cradle. I had to put him back into bed."

She turned as she heard the door opening. "Morning, Jack. I was just telling Dad about last night. D'you remember?"

"Yes. I was freezing."

"I'm not surprised. Have you seen the snow out there? It can't have let up all night."

The snow! He'd forgotten the snow. He ran to the back door and tugged it open. So thick! He'd never seen it so thick before. But now the storm was spent and just the tiniest of flakes were falling thinly.

"Hey, it's brilliant! Brilliant! Brilliant!" He shut the door and danced round the kitchen.

"Be careful! You'll knock everything over." His father's growls came from behind the newspaper.

Jack sat down and helped himself to a slice of toast. There was newly made marmalade, gleaming orange.

"Mmm, this is brilliant."

"Everything's brilliant this morning, apparently."

His father's morning tongue was as sharp as the marmalade. Jack ignored it. He watched the reflection of the light as it glinted on his knife. He remembered another knife, in another kitchen.

"D'you know if there's a place called Eyam?" Jack felt as if his life depended on the answer.

"Yes, it's about an hour's drive from here. Haven't you done it at school?"

"Done it?"

"It's a really interesting place. I must take you there sometime. In sixteen hundred and something there was a . . . Oh drat!"

The ringing of the phone pierced the warmth of the kitchen. His mother stood up.

"Hi, Alison. No, no, you're not interrupting anything."

"Yes she is! Tell her to go away!"

"Jack!" His mother covered the mouthpiece and glared at him. His father lowered the morning paper and glared at him. Jack glared at them both.

Not interrupting anything! Huh! He put his chin in his hands and examined his half-eaten toast gloomily. A phone call from Alison could last all morning. He pushed his chair away from the table.

"Finish your breakfast, Jack." Dad folded his newspaper and drained the last of his tea.

"I've had enough, thanks."

"Don't forget to clean your teeth," whispered Mum, cupping the mouthpiece again.

Chance would be a fine thing!

Chapter 4
The Wakes

The sky was a sulky grey, low as the chimney pots. The milkman had left the gate open and stamped his black footprints in the snow. Beyond the gate, cars churned up the dirty slush with a noise that sizzled deliciously in Jack's ears. He walked down the path, placing his feet in the milkman's footprints so that he wouldn't spoil the snow. No doubt Dad would ruin the back path on his way to the garage.

Jack thought back to the events of the previous evening and knew that he could not explain them. However unlikely any other explanation might be, he knew that he had not been dreaming. One thing was for sure: the place existed. Mum had heard of it.

He remembered a mural on the side of an old pub in town. Some people were carrying a banner which said, Knowledge is power. Yes it is, he thought. Knowledge is power. If I knew what was happening to me; if I understood, then I could do something.

There it was again; that strange feeling that there was something he must do. As though some task had been set for him. But what task? What was it that he was supposed to do?

He trudged up Tom's path and knocked on the door. It was hurled open with a bang and there was Tom, putting his sweatshirt on with one hand and holding a bacon sandwich with the other. His hair looked as though it was trying to escape from his head.

"Overslept," he mumbled.

His dishevelled state did nothing to spoil his charms as far as the girls were concerned though. Two of Tom's admirers passed the house as the boys opened the gate.

"Hi," said one, and giggled. The other one examined the snow and blushed.

Some people thought Tom was the best-looking boy in the school. Tom agreed with them. He pushed his hands through his hair and said, "Hi, girls."

Jack wondered what it would be like to have girls giggling over him. Tom seemed to enjoy it. He pushed his glasses further up his nose and pretended not to notice.

He had thought it best not to say anything about Eyam. Tom would only come up with some practical explanation that was all wrong.

But he just had to talk to somebody; and Tom was his friend.

They were at school by the time Jack had finished his story, and Tom had listened silently; nodded occasionally.

"It was just a dream though, Jack. Stands to reason."

"But there really is a place called Eyam. Mum's heard of it."

"You must have read about it, years ago, and forgotten it until now."

Perhaps he's right, Jack thought; it's a good explanation. But it doesn't feel right. And it doesn't explain how I could dream about a girl I'd never seen before. Or about the cradle.

"Oh no!" Jack thumped his forehead.

"What's the matter?" Tom was holding open the cloakroom door and the five-to-nine bell was ringing.

"They're taking the cradle back. I'm going home."

"Don't be stupid."

But he'd gone.

Jack threw open the door. His breaths came in painful gasps and his feet burned with hot aches.

"Jack! What on earth are you doing here?" His mother looked up from the book she was reading.

"Has it gone yet?"

"What?"

"The cradle," Jack shouted. "You're not taking it back. I won't let you."

His mother started to laugh.

"It's not funny!"

"I'm sorry, Jack." She put the book down. "We're not taking it back."

"But Dad said."

"Oh, you know what Dad's like. Full of hot air and minor explosions. It's all forgotten by the next day."

Jack felt like kicking something. Pity Dad wasn't around.

"So I've skived off school for nothing then?"

"Yes, I'm afraid you have."

"Hmph." He glowered at her.

"Have some tea. It's just made." She poured tea into a mug and pushed it towards him.

Jack bent his face over it and let the steam seep into his skin, moist and warm. He began to relax. His glasses steamed up and he lifted his face to look at his mother.

"Bit foggy in here."

She laughed and Jack felt suddenly happy. He looked at his mother with her mug balanced on the bump; her built-in table she called it. He wished that things could stay like this for ever.

"How long before the baby's born?"

"Soon. Three weeks or so."

"Only three more weeks by ourselves then."

She smiled and reached across to stroke his hair. Jack looked down at his tea and ran his finger round the rim of the mug.

"When are you going back to work?"

"When the baby's about six months old."

"I wish you could stay at home always. I like you being home."

"What, just so that I can be here when you decide to abscond from school? What am I supposed to do all day?"

"Look after me and Dad and the baby."

"You're beginning to sound just like my mother, Jack Rutherford. There's more to life than loading a washing machine you know." Her voice was teasing, but Jack knew she was serious.

"I know."

"Well, young man, I suppose I'd better phone school and make soothing noises about your late arrival."

School happened and that was about all that could be said for it. A bad start to the day usually meant the rest of the day went badly too. And it had. Jack's mind had been elsewhere of course, the fact that his body was at school seemed unimportant. He'd longed for bedtime so that he could be alone; so that he could decide whether he had enough courage to try again.

And now it was bedtime and he was afraid. He reached out and touched the carved acorn; turned it gingerly. No! He pulled his fingers back; put them in his pocket out of harm's way. He couldn't. He could not. He daren't try again. He was at home. He was safe. Going to Eyam could be dangerous.

But there was another feeling. A feeling that battled with the fear and overcame it. A feeling that robbed him of choice; that forced him, compelled him to turn the acorn. He turned it once, twice. It turned easily. Darkness swirled around his head and he felt himself being sucked into a long black tunnel. Then the whispers, more urgent than before, "Jack, Jack, Jack."

"Keep still child. Fidget, fidget, fidget." Mrs Roe was looking through Susannah's hair and picking things out of it. Like Nitty Norah, the Head Explorer, thought Jack. Bet she's got nits.

Jack sat down on the stairs. A door opened off from the kitchen and he could see a group of people sitting round a table; two men and a woman, laughing and talking. The air danced with excitement.

William jerked around the kitchen in a long white dress which threatened to trip him up.

Jack smiled at him, smiled at the kitchen,

smiled at the girl, who had not yet seen him. Strangely, he was no longer afraid. The only thing that mattered to him now was to be here.

"I am here because I want to be here. I chose to come, I can choose when to go back. I am in control." Jack murmured the words, like an incantation. "I am in control."

Despite his confidence though, something held him back from leaving the stairs. On his last visit only the girl had seen him. But he had no way of knowing if that would be the case this time. Rules that he had taken for granted had been broken. Jack didn't know what the rules were any more; anything could happen. Perhaps he wasn't in control after all.

"Now, go show your family what a pretty young lady you are."

Jack watched the girl glide into the next room. She twirled and curtsied elegantly.

"Do you like it, Uncle John?"

"Indeed I do, my girl. What say you Elizabeth?"

"She looks like a queen; does she not?" Aunt Elizabeth bent forward and felt the shiny material, rubbing it between thumb and forefinger.

"We shall miss all the merrymaking if we admire Susannah's dress much longer. And I am most anxious to see the mummers' play." The man who spoke was small and thin with a grey beard covering most of his face. Deep blue eyes moved rapidly and gave life to the face.

"Oh, Father. Do you not care for my dress?"

"Yes, Susannah. It is the most beautiful dress in the world. And you are the second most beautiful girl; after your mother."

"Oh, Joshua." Mrs Roe banged her husband on the arm and grinned.

He needs his eyes testing, thought Jack. If I had a face like that, I'd have it ironed.

He turned as William, alone in the kitchen, gave a loud screech. The little boy was teetering towards the open fire. One more step and he'd be in it."

"Hot. Hot," he chanted happily. He stretched his short arms towards a black pot, suspended above the fire. Jack looked at the gossiping family. They had forgotten William.

Jack ran across the room and grabbed the little boy under both arms. As he stepped backwards, he knocked over a wooden stool which clattered noisily onto the stone floor. William screamed.

There was a rush of bodies into the kitchen. Mrs Roe lunged at Jack and pulled William from his arms. The girl raised her hands to her mouth and Jack saw that she was trembling. Her father pushed past her, followed by Aunt Elizabeth and Uncle John.

"What ails you, Hannah? Calm yourself." Mr

Roe took William and steered his wife to a chair. She sat down heavily. Her voice came in sobs.

"The child, Joshua. The child. Praise God he is safe. He was in the air. There must be demons in the house. We must get Parson Mompesson to pray for us."

Demons indeed! I'll give 'em demons, thought Jack. "He nearly fell in the fire!" His voice rang round the room, but only Susannah heard. She looked at him, still trembling.

"I tell you he was floating in the air, Joshua. Floating in the air."

"Hush, wife. You are exhausted with all the stitching and baking these past days. You are not yourself."

"I am perfectly myself." She stood up quietly and wiped her eyes. "Come. Let us go. We shall be late."

Jack followed the group out of the house. The girl seemed eager to get through the door quickly, to get as far away from Jack as possible. But she turned, as the rest of her family carried on up the street and said, as if she found the fact unbelievable, "You saved William."

"Saved William, saved William, saved William." Eerie voices echoed in Jack's head. He felt dizzy. Everywhere was black. Stars moved across a black sky. White faces swirled through the heavens, chanting, "Saved William, saved William." They disappeared through a closing door: the door with no handle.

He shook his head. Slowly the dizziness eased and the girl's face came back into focus, watching him still. He screwed up his eyes at the bright sunlight.

"What ails you, boy?"

"Nothing. I'm all right." He shook his head. What in the world was happening to him? What was it all about?

Eyam was crowded. Carts rumbled and heaved up the hill and people shouted to one another as they recognised friends and acquaintances from other villages. Jack trailed behind the rest of the family, becoming so caught up with all the colour and activity that the unanswered questions slipped to the back of his mind.

Cottage doors were open wide to the sunlight. An old woman stood in the doorway of one of them and the family stopped as she spoke.

"'Tis wondrous fine weather, praise the Lord."

"Indeed, Mistress Jennings."

Nobody spoke to Jack.

They came to a church with a square tower. It looked as though it had been there always, set down by a giant hand alongside the cottages, each a part of the other. Everything belonged; everything fitted.

The trees in the churchyard were hung with garlands, and small posies of flowers had been set up at the edge of the street. Obviously some sort of carnival, thought Jack; connected with the church, by the look of things.

"For shame! 'Tis a heathen practice to trade in front of the church. Parson Stanley would not have allowed such things, wakes or no wakes." Mrs Roe pulled a white cloth from her sleeve and mopped her face.

"Indeed, Hannah," said Uncle John, "But Parson Mompesson forgets, perhaps, that our Lord turned the tables of the traders and moneylenders."

"But these stalls are beyond the church walls, Mother. Surely it is not the same thing at all?"

"Hush, child! Do not argue with your elders and betters."

Susannah turned and pulled a face behind her mother's back. She caught Jack's eye, stuck her nose in the air, and turned her back on him.

"Not scared of me any more, Susannah? Susannah Roe, is it? Safety in numbers, eh?"

"Go away."

"Friendly little soul, aren't you?"

Jack dropped a little way back from the group. Not too far though; he didn't want to get lost in the crowd.

He sniffed at the air. A delicious smell wafted above the smell of pressed-in bodies. A Sunday dinner smell. Jack sniffed in ecstasy. It seemed ages since he'd eaten. A gap appeared in the crowd and Jack saw two men turning the handles of an enormous spit on which hung a whole cow, or so it seemed, dripping with fat. The fat hissed and exploded in the fire.

The street widened out onto a green and the crowds thronged more thickly, in their yellows and blues, reds and greens. Stallholders shouted their wares and acrobats in orange tunics tumbled to the music of a fiddler. But above all this, yet woven into it like golden thread in a tapestry, was the sun. It beat down in pulses of throbbing heat.

Jack gazed at the stalls in fascination. There were herbs and spices, breads and cakes, ribbons, cheeses. The smells were sun-warmed and sharp, pungent and sweet. He closed his eyes again and breathed deeply. And then, as he opened them, everything became clear to him; everything fell into place. He understood why he had come to Eyam; understood that he had been sent for, that he had a job to do. And then the moment was gone. He struggled to grasp it again, like a half-remembered dream.

But it would not come back. The harder he tried, the further it slipped away, elusive and tantalising. He knew no more than before.

A large circle was forming on the grass and a fiddler was striking up a tune. Jack saw Susannah; part of the circle with her father and Uncle John.

No one, except the girl, knew that he was there, and he felt a sudden urgent defiance against the strange events surrounding him. He, Jack Rutherford, would be the one to decide what he would and would not do. With a rush of exhilaration, he ducked under the joined hands and into the middle of the circle. Country dancing was not one of Jack's favourite hobbies, but for some reason he felt that, just for today, there was nothing he would like better.

The dancers skipped sideways, unaware of the boy in their midst. He twirled experimentally and looked around him. No one was looking; no one had seen.

He felt a surge of power at his invisibility and laughed out loud. He caught the girl's eye and she gave him a look of utter amazement. Then she was trying hard not to laugh, but the corners of her mouth twitched and she had to look away from him.

He stood on tiptoe and turned round and round, fluttering his fingers in tiny movements, pretending to be a girl, but looking like a lumpy boy. He leaped and cavorted, gathering speed in time to the music. Then he stopped, put out his tongue at the onlookers, pulled a face like a gargoyle. No one could see him. It was magic!

"Roll up! Roll up! Come and see the finest show in all England. Come hear news of the king and his parliament. Be you all astonished at the skill of the jugglers and acrobats. Let mirth take away the cares from your brow." The jester bowed, and scurried like a bent mouse, into a tent with orange and yellow stripes.

The crowd trickled slowly towards a grassy mound. They sat in small groups, laughing and gossiping, absorbed in the atmosphere of happiness that seeped into every blade of grass, every stone, every person in the village.

Jack squeezed in beside Susannah who sat with the rest of her family with William on her knee. He turned his face to Jack and beamed at him.

"Boy, boy," he said, pointing his finger. Jack pushed his glasses further up his nose and beamed back.

"He can see you." Susannah's voice was quiet, incredulous.

"My name's Jack, not boy. Are you listening,

monster?" He put his finger in the little boy's outstretched hand. William drew it slowly into his mouth and bit it.

"Ouch!" Jack rubbed his finger and grinned.

"Then I am not possessed. William sees you too." Susannah breathed out slowly, heavily; a sigh of enormous relief. "Praise God I am not possessed. I am not."

"Course you're not. I could have told you that, any day."

Her eyes were bright with unshed tears, and as she bent her head to William's, they spilled out and fell, wetting the little boy's cap. She sobbed as though her heart would break.

Jack wriggled uncomfortably. What could he say?

"All that talk about witches and possession; it's just rubbish." That would make her feel better.

"Do you not understand, boy?" The girl wiped her eyes on her sleeve, vehemently. "The devil has many evil doings."

Anybody would think it was the Dark Ages, the way she's going on, thought Jack. Nobody believes in the devil any more, do they; or witches? But he said nothing.

There was so much he wanted to talk to her about, to ask her. But a drum roll was announcing the start of the show. Heads turned, bottoms ceased fidgeting, chattering stopped. It would have to wait.

The mummers performed a play which Jack didn't understand, there being lots of jokes about the king and parliament. But the crowd clapped enthusiastically at every trip and twirl, noisily enjoying themselves.

And then it was over. The jester bowed and held his arms outstretched, to the crowd.

"Good people of Eyam,
Our show is done,
We must bid you farewell."

He swept his arms in a wide arc, and then brought them back to the front again, palms upturned.

"The sun shines on your village today.
Happiness and peace abound
And you are at one with your neighbours.
God smiles on you.
But heed the wise man.
Loiter not in a fool's paradise."

The jester put a mask to his face. It was a skull with black gaping eye sockets, its teeth clamped in a macabre grin. Silver tears spilled over the cheekbones.

"The sun will dip beneath the world.

The dark will come
And your faces will be changed
As day becomes night.
Your joy will turn to sorrow.
The jester shall jest no more.
Good day to you all."

The mood of the crowd changed instantly. There were boos and hisses and mutters of "shame". Jack felt something black roll into his heart and lodge there, like a stone.

Chapter 5
In the Churchyard

Jack opened his eyes. Nothing in his bedroom had changed. Everything was the same, yet everything was different. He felt as though he'd come back from a long journey; all the ordinary, everyday things were like shadows, not real any more.

He picked up his glasses and went to the bathroom. A bright red face stared back at him from the mirror. Jack touched his cheeks with both hands and stroked his face. Perhaps he'd got a fever. He scratched the back of his neck thoughtfully. Ouch! He turned and looked over his shoulder into the mirror. His neck was even redder than his face. He looked down at his arms: red. He groaned out loud: "How are you going to get out of this one, Jack Rutherford? Sunburned in February." He scowled at his reflection. Red hair, red skin, red boy; red for danger, when Mum finds out!

Jack dragged out a red jumper from the bottom of his wardrobe. Tom said it made him look like a red pepper with glasses and he'd not worn it since. But he was going to wear it now, for camouflage.

It didn't work. Mum was in the kitchen, eating toast and looking dangerously alert.

"What's wrong with your face?"

"It's ugly."

"Apart from that. Come here. " She put her hand on his forehead. "You're hot. Open your mouth."

"Oh, Mum, forget you're a doctor for once."

"Open your mouth." She put down her toast and wiped her hands.

Jack opened his mouth.

"Mmm, nothing there."

"Nothing? You mean my tongue's gone?"

"No, unfortunately."

He pulled away. He made for the toaster and put in two slices of extra thick toasting bread.

"Let me look at your neck." Mum made a grab for the back of his jumper.

"No!"

"You're sunburned!"

"No, I'm not."

"Yes, you are. Have you been on a sunbed?" The words came out slowly, in surprise.

"Yes. Somebody at school's got one." Jack took the escape route gratefully. Why hadn't he thought of it?

"Who? Just you tell me who and I'll be on that phone to their parents." Her chin jutted forward like it always did when she was angry. Except that she wasn't angry; she was furious.

"Nobody you know." Now I've done it, he thought. She's not going to let go till she's drawn blood.

"Just you tell me whose sunbed. Now!"

"I can't, can I? I'm not going to grass on them."

"Tell me, Jack."

"No. I can't."

"Well, if you ever go on one again, there's going to be big, big trouble. Understood?"

Jack grunted.

"Don't you realise how dangerous those things can be?"

Oh, stop going on about it, he thought.

"Don't ever do this again. Look at the state you're in."

Her stare seemed to reach inside him and he blushed under the sunburn.

She gave him one last, disapproving look and picked up the morning paper. Whew! That was a near thing.

On the way home from school, Jack realised that his own doubts had all but disappeared: you don't get sunburn from dreams, he'd told himself. Tom had been really impressed when he'd shown him, but he'd stuck to the sunbed story when the rest of the lads had noticed. They'd been playing five a side in the gym at the time, and the games teacher had said that, in his opinion, Jack needed his head looking at. Jack had agreed with him.

So his mood was confident as he strode up the back path, and he was determined to tackle Mum about Eyam. He'd had plenty of opportunity since yesterday morning's telephone call but had felt uneasy. Now was the time to do it. Seize the moment!

But the moment had already been seized; by Alison. She and Mum were having one of their deep conversations again. Jack wasn't sure whether to kick her on the shins or tell her to go home; right now! He suspected that neither approach would be popular, so he contented himself with glaring at Alison and ignoring Mum.

"What's the matter with you? Had maths all day or something?" Mum obviously thought this was funny.

Jack didn't bother to reply; just slung his bag across the floor so that it made a hissing noise like skates on ice.

"Your mother's been spring cleaning. That mean's the baby won't be long." Alison looked smug, as if she knew the secrets of the universe but wasn't telling.

"Oh, Alison, honestly! I've got another three weeks to go yet."

Jack slammed out of the kitchen. She's an old witch, an old hag. I hate her! We've got three weeks; three whole weeks. And she's trying to take them off me. I hate her!

He flung open his bedroom door and pulled a piece of paper from his notebook. "Alison's a wally," he wrote all over it. He drew a picture of Alison wearing a witch's hat and stuck it on the bedroom door where Mum would see it. He felt much better.

Later that night, when he should have been asleep, he stood by the cradle. He felt his stomach contract as he reached out his hand. His breathing was loud in the midnight room, grew louder as the acorn turned. He wanted to stop: but it was too late. He felt himself drawn once more through a long black tunnel filled with voices. The voices whispered his name. They were talking about him.

The family was seated around the table, having a meal. The girl sat opposite her parents, who had their backs to the stairs. William peered over his mother's shoulder.

"Boy, Boy," he screamed.

Susannah's head jerked upwards. She rose from her seat and sat down again, knocking her plate on to the floor with a clang of metal on stone.

"Mercy, child! What ails you these days?" The mother tutted and fussed until the plate, the bread and the cheese had been piled back on to the table. Susannah sat down with a burning face and downcast eyes.

"Boy. Boy." William bounced excitedly and pointed his finger at Jack. "Boy!"

"What is it, William? There is no boy." The woman smiled and shook her little son playfully.

Exhilaration surged through Jack's body like a moving force. He could travel to Eyam and back as often as he wanted. And he was free to do as he liked because he couldn't be seen. Endless possibilities lay before him. He was invisible!

But Mrs Roe was not happy. She shook her head. "This house is strange of late. I am not easy in it." She looked round the kitchen, her head tucked into her shoulder like a tortoise's, as if she were afraid of seeing something that shouldn't be there.

"It's only me," said Jack, with his hand on the father's shoulder. "Nothing to worry about at all." He patted him on the head and did a silly walk round the kitchen. Susannah giggled.

"What has become of you, child? You smirk

when there is nought to smirk about and behave most oddly."

"I am sorry, Mother. I think I am in need of air. May I go out?"

"Not so hasty. We have not thanked the Lord yet. Joshua?"

Heads bowed and Mr Roe said grace: "We thank thee, Lord, for thy bountiful provision. Amen."

Half an hour later they sat in a lane, high above Eyam. Below them they could see thatched cottage roofs and the square tower of the church. It was hot and William toddled about, pulling at grass and picking up stones. He walked towards his sister with teetering steps. He wavered unsteadily for a second and then fell on to his bottom with a bump. He began to cry so Susannah picked him up and sat him on her knee.

"D'you mind looking after William?"

"Of course not." The girl seemed astounded by the question. "It is my duty. And he is an angel, is he not?"

William struggled from his sister's knee and scrabbled in the dirt. Perhaps angel was going a bit far, thought Jack, but he nodded anyway because he knew that Susannah's friendship was all thanks to the little boy. If William hadn't been able to see him, then Susannah might still think she was possessed. He lay back against a stone wall and closed his eyes, drowsy and contented in the sun.

"Yes, he is an angel," Susannah continued. "I often think of my three brothers who died and I am so thankful for William."

"What?" He sat up and frowned at her. "Are you joking?"

"Would I jest about such a matter?" She played with the strings of her bonnet, one eye on William who was shouting at a thrush.

"But three?"

"But three, Jack. What is so strange about that?"

"My Gran's dead, but she's the only one I know who is."

"But many children die as babes. You surely know some?"

"No, I don't."

"You are a strange manner of boy. I never saw nor heard anyone like you before."

"Well, babies don't usually die where I come from."

Susannah said nothing. Jack could see that she didn't understand. And he felt some of her old wariness return; as if she didn't quite trust him.

"And where do you come from, Master Jack?"

Jack caught the mockery in her voice. He

stood up and began to walk slowly down the lane. The girl strode after him.

"Well, Jack? Where *do* you come from?"

He stopped, sat down again, and hung his head between his knees. Where do I come from and where do I come to? Where *do* I come to? He looked at the earth beneath his feet. Earth baked dry in the Eyam sun. He came to Eyam, of course. Eyam where there are real people, and where there is real earth. He looked at William and his sister, then picked up a pebble, hurled it with all his strength, watching it rise and fall, then disappear into a clump of grass.

William hurried on down the lane, lurching from side to side like a penguin. Susannah watched her brother silently, torn between the need to follow him and her fascination with Jack who seemed to be somewhere else, beyond her reach.

And where is Eyam? Jack answered his own question: Eyam is here, all around me. But if I had a map of the world, where would I find Eyam? If I had a history of the world, where would Eyam fit in? When is Eyam? It didn't make sense yet somehow seemed to be the right question: when is Eyam?

"Where is Eyam, Susannah?"

"Here, boy. Eyam is here, all around us." Her words echoed his own. "Where else could it be? We are in Eyam."

"I know that. That's not what I mean."

Susannah looked puzzled, but William's small figure was disappearing fast and there was no time to reply.

He heard William scream in delight as his sister chased after him; watched him run even faster in his funny penguin gait. Jack caught up with them as Susannah swung the little boy up into her arms, the two of them giggling breathlessly.

"I mean, is it the Eyam in Derbyshire? Or are we in Yorkshire, or Hampshire, or America?"

"Derby is a long way from here," said Susannah. "And I do not know these other places you speak of."

Honestly! How come the stupid girl hadn't even heard of America? "Well, what year is it then?" Jack's voice was impatient.

"It is the year of our Lord, 1665." She recited the words carefully, as if they had been deliberately committed to memory.

"1665? 1665?"

"What did you expect, boy?"

What had he expected? The nonsensical answer made sense of all the other nonsensical things about Eyam. 1665! Just wait till he told Tom. 1665!

"What did you expect?" Her voice was quiet, persistent.

"This is 1665. Right?"

"Indeed. I have just said so."

"Well, where I come from, it's 1992. Turn the numbers upside down and we're nearly back here again."

Jack looked straight ahead. The lane curved and there was a stone cottage on the bend with a pigpen at the side and hens nodding in the garden. The countryside shimmered in the heat. Out of the corner of his eye, he could see Susannah looking at him, her pink face filmy with perspiration.

"The year of our Lord, 1992." She said it softly, almost to herself. "Three hundred and twenty-seven years."

"Brilliant," said Jack, who was hopeless at maths.

"Numbers are simple, full of sense. But these numbers do not make sense. The year of our Lord, 1992 has not yet happened." She looked at Jack and shook her head, as if he were beyond all understanding.

They were back in the village. Susannah put William down.

"I cannot carry you any longer, little brother. My arms are breaking." She picked up the hem of her apron and wiped her face. "And my brain is in pieces." She smiled at Jack. "You may come and see the grave of my three brothers, if you wish."

Jack liked the churchyard. There was a

sundial on the wall of the church with roman numerals and words written in Latin: at least he thought they were Latin. He looked at it for ages, before realising that Susannah had disappeared behind the back of the church.

"Hey, wait for me."

She was kneeling on a grassy mound in front of a small grey stone. She held a round earthenware pot with tiny blue flowers in it. The grubby white of her apron formed a backcloth to them. She was praying. There was not the smallest sound. Even William was quiet.

Susannah looked up as Jack knelt beside her. The headstone was carved with ornate, sloping letters which told of the beloved sons of Joshua and Hannah Roe, and the much loved brothers of Susannah. There was a verse from the bible: Suffer little children to come unto me. Then the names, one after the other.

Joshua, aged 6 weeks.
Abel, aged 4 years and 3 months.
Samuel, aged 9 months.

"We are fortunate to have such a stone."

Jack said nothing. He couldn't think of anything to say. Three dead brothers and she thought she was lucky.

William looked solemnly at Jack, as if he

knew his thoughts and agreed with them. "Chack," he said, softly.

"Abel was my special one. He looked like William and was such a Jack-a-dandy. My little Abe. One day he ran into the . . ."

"Good day, Susannah."

A shadow fell across them. Jack turned quickly. The man looked like a domino, he thought; all in black with two dots of white at collar and cuff. He was tall, with a wide-brimmed hat and eyes so heavy and large they seemed to spill from their lids. His socks looked itchy. Jack would have refused to wear them.

"Parson Mompesson." Susannah jumped up and gathered William to her. "I came to see my brothers' grave."

"Praise God they are in His care." The parson nodded to Susannah and glided away.

"He looks like a big crow," said Jack, who was sitting on the grass still.

"That is disrespectful, Jack."

"It's true."

"I am quite overcome when I am in his presence. But he is a good, kind man."

The parson disappeared into the church porch. Jack heard a door creak and the thud of an iron knocker on wood.

"OK, let's go."

"What is OK?"

"It means yes."

"Well, why do you not say yes, then?" She pointed to his glasses. "Strange objects, strange dress, strange speech. Why do you come here? To mock me?" She ran after William who was trying to uproot a rock, and walked back, looking hot and miserable.

"I haven't come to mock you." He turned away at the sight of her face, closed and angry. What had brought this on? All he'd said was OK.

"You do not have to try seemingly. 'Tis easy for you."

Jack walked off quickly. If that's what she thought, he wasn't going to argue. He'd go back home and forget about her and her stuck up ways. The five minute friendship was over.

Susannah overtook him, her back stiff with anger, her strides long under the folds of her brown woollen dress. Well, she could please herself.

William had fallen asleep on his sister's shoulder and his blond curls strayed damply from under his cap. Jack put out a hand and touched his head. At least William hadn't fallen out with him.

He followed Susannah into the cottage and went upstairs without speaking. If that's how she felt, there was no point in coming back again.

He turned the acorn roughly. And then he was falling into a whirling, whispering blackness that reached out to him and sucked him into itself.

Susannah Roe could go hang.

Chapter 6
Talking about Time

"What would you do, Tom?"

Tom leaned backwards, his heels slicing through the thin layer of slush as the swing juddered forwards. He pushed it back again with the tips of his toes, taking small steps, like a ballet dancer on points. Over and over again.

"Tom?" Jack sat on the next swing, still as a rabbit; straining for an answer.

"I s'pose I'd go back if I was that bothered about it."

Jack leaned his cheek against the cold chain and swung gently from side to side. Tom's answer satisfied him and he smiled to himself. It was, of course, the only answer; the cradle called to him wherever he was. He couldn't ignore it.

"C'mon let's go; I'm freezing and my bum's wet." Tom leaped off the swing which snaked from side to side with a clank of metal. He slapped at the seat of his pants where the melted snow had left a dark stain.

The two boys walked in silence through the park. Dogs barked, children screamed, parents shouted. The snow had lost its crunch and lay in soft patches with blades of grass poking through. Jack watched a dog lift its leg against a tree trunk, causing a patch of snow to melt away into a yellow-edged hole.

"I will go back, Tom. I don't think I could stay away even if I wanted to."

"Back to your ghosts. Good idea."

"I don't believe in ghosts."

"Some people wouldn't believe what's happening to you."

Jack shrugged his shoulders.

The afternoon was turning to evening. A drift of people headed towards them, homeward bound. He knew his world was different from theirs; knew he had secrets they would never believe, even if he could tell them.

"I bet nobody will ever really believe me."

"Does it matter?"

"Of course it matters. Just think, Tom, it could change the way the whole world thinks about time. Scientists would have to think again."

"I can just see the newspapers," said Tom, waving his arms about. "Jack Rutherford, boy wonder from Derby, turns the world of science upside down."

Jack thumped Tom, who ran off. Jack caught him and tackled him from behind, bringing them both down in a patch of mud and slush. Tom lay on the ground, moaning and clutching various bits of his body in quick succession.

"Get up you foul and hideous fiend, else I plunge you with my sword." Jack brandished an imaginary weapon in the air.

"Have mercy, my lord, have mercy." Tom groaned and writhed dramatically.

"OK, audition over, you get the part. Two hundred a week and as much free coke as you can drink. Arise, Sir Tom."

Sir Tom arose. "Look at my clothes, Jack Rutherford. My mum'll kill me."

"Oh, diddums then. Tommy's been a naughty little boy and his mummy's going to smack his bottom. Don't cry, Tommy, Mummy'll kiss you better when she's over it."

Tom swung a punch in Jack's direction. Jack ducked.

"I'm starving. Hope there's something nice for tea. I could just eat strawberry jam with loads of strawberries in it."

"And peanut butter," said Tom.

"Yuck," said Jack.

The two boys came through the park gates, and walked on under the darkening sky. The huge black skeleton of an oak tree towered above them and Jack could see a crescent moon, half-hidden, through its branches. Sleek black leaves poked through the snow, varnished by the light of a street lamp.

Jack thrust his hands deep in his pockets and bent his head against the rising wind.

"Tom, I've been thinking about this time business."

"Have you?" said Tom, in mock surprise. Jack ignored him.

"If none of my own time, twentieth century time, passes while I'm in Eyam, then I could stay there for ever, couldn't I?"

"Could you?" Tom sounded doubtful.

"Yes, I think I could. And listen to this."

Tom listened.

"I could stay there until it got to be our own time again."

"How?"

"Well, I think I'd stay a boy forever; not grow any older."

Tom kicked at a pile of snow-sodden leaves. "How come?"

"Because none of my own time is passing. Whenever I come back from Eyam, I find I've only been away a few seconds. And I should only age in my own time, shouldn't I?"

"I don't see how that follows."

Jack didn't reply at once. He had to make his thoughts absolutely clear so that he could explain things properly. Not that it would need much explanation if Tom would just listen for once.

"Well, it's simple enough."

"How do you know that something won't go wrong and you do get older; become a wrinkly overnight or something? Tom hobbled like an old man, and croaked: "Tom, it's me. Remember me? Your old mate, Jack?"

Jack laughed.

"I bet it'd be dead boring. Just imagine, all the people you knew in Eyam, like Susannah and William, would grow old and die. Then you'd be left on your own, not knowing anyone."

Jack hadn't thought of that. "I'd know Susannah's children and grandchildren and great-grandchildren. It'd be fantastic, knowing a family through generations and generations. I could tell the young ones all about their ancestors from first hand. Be a sort of family historian."

"Fantastic and not possible. It's fantasy, Jack. Fantasy."

Jack decided not to hear this. He went on, "Anyway, what I was going to say is: I don't age, so I stay there until it gets to be now again."

"Yes?"

"Then I come home and I've been born again

and I meet my other self. There'd be two of me, you see. The one that's born now, me in other words, and the me who'd be born when it got to be my birthday again. Like an action replay of time." Jack's voice ended on a note of triumph.

Tom said nothing for a while. Jack, waiting for an answer, watched him run his hands along some iron railings. Remembered how, when they were little, they used to run past this house because they thought it was haunted.

"Don't be daft."

"Eh?"

"Don't be daft. Stop being a wally. Pull yourself together." Tom recited the phrases slowly, as if Jack were stupid and needed to have things explained to him.

"What's daft about it? It could happen."

"Yeah, and my Grandma's a Viking."

"You've got no imagination, that's your trouble."

"Imagination's the right word," Tom muttered.

Jack was speechless. This was Tom talking. Tom, his best friend. Tom, who was now letting him down.

"I'm sorry, Jack, but would you believe me if things were the other way round?"

"I don't know."

"No. Well, see you then."

"See you."

The first flurries of new snow were just beginning and Tom's tongue was extended to its limits, trying to catch the soft, cold flakes. He walked on, head twisted to the sky, lost in the demands of his task.

Jack watched his friend disappear beyond the light of the street lamp. Tom has no idea, he thought, no idea at all what this means to me. You'd think he'd at least make an effort to believe me, at least try. He made his way to the back door.

Jack went to the off-licence after tea. He bought the biggest bar of chocolate he could afford, as a sort of peace offering for Susannah. It might help to cement things. Chocolate cement; he smiled at the thought. She might trust him again if they could share something solid. Solid, chocolate cement. He laughed out loud.

Later that evening, Jack looked out of the window to see the snow falling, just as it had been the first time. He looked at the cradle. It seemed so innocent: an ordinary wooden crib. Yet it had reached out to him in a dream; had called to him from a shop window. Why?

If it had a purpose in taking him to Eyam, why wasn't it clear? And if there wasn't a purpose, what was the sense of it all? One thing only was clear: he could not stay away from Eyam.

Jack picked up his father's heavy black torch: it might be useful. He patted his jeans pocket; the chocolate was there.

He twisted the acorn and was hurled into a falling blackness. "Jack, Jack, Jack." The chanting rhythm grew louder; the whispers turned to screams. "Help, Jack; help, Jack; help, Jack."

There was a thud as Jack came to. He dropped the torch and it rolled noisily across the wooden floorboards. He muttered furiously under his breath, hoping no one had heard.

But someone had. Someone came panting up the stairs. Jack picked up the torch and pushed it under Susannah's bed.

Mrs Roe poked her head round the door.

"Nothing is amiss, the Lord be praised, but I can not think what caused such commotion."

"Thunder, I'll lay wager."

"Indeed, you'll not lay wager, my girl. This is a God-fearing house."

"'Tis but a saying, Mother."

"Aye, and the devil's at that."

Susannah squeezed past her mother and shivered when she saw Jack. Then she smiled.

"What is it, child? Is something amiss?"

"No, Mother. 'Tis raining, that is all."

81

Mrs Roe looked sharply at her daughter. "It has been raining these three days, Lady Roe."

"Yes, but see how swiftly it falls this minute." Susannah turned round and round towards the window, her brown dress twirling.

Her mother headed for the stairs, tutting loudly.

Susannah ran up to Jack; so close that she almost trod on his toes. Jack stepped back. She stank!

But she didn't seem to notice the boy's sour face. "I thought you would not come back. 'Tis seven days since last you came."

"Is it?" Funny, thought Jack, I could have sworn it was only yesterday.

"Forgive me for my bad behaviour last time. My wicked temper burns like fire at times. Mother says I shall die for it."

Charming! thought Jack. But he said, "That's all right," as if he hadn't given it much thought. "Look, I've brought you a present."

"A present!" Susannah grinned and turned pink. She took the chocolate bar and sat down on the bed. She ran her fingers across the wrapping and turned the bar over in her hands. "What is it?"

"Chocolate."

Susannah unwrapped the silver paper slowly and put the chocolate on the bed. "Oh, it is beautiful." She lifted the shiny wrapping so that it caught the light, blue and silver. "Oh, it is beautiful. Thank you, Jack."

"That's not it, dafthead. It's the chocolate." He pointed at it, "You're supposed to eat it."

"Oh."

"Go on, it's delicious."

She lifted the chocolate to her face and smelled it. Then she dabbed her fingers onto the tiny grains that had fallen loose from the bar, and put her finger into her mouth.

Her blue eyes opened wide and then closed. "Mmm. It is wonderful."

Jack showed her how to break the chocolate into squares and they shared it between them.

"I declare that I have never tasted such delight before. Not even Mother's spice cakes."

"Susannah! Come and eat, girl." Mrs Roe's powerful voice echoed up the stairs.

"I must go."

Whatever they were about to eat smelled good. Good job he'd eaten the chocolate or he'd be starving by now. It occurred to him that hopping about in different times and places was probably a bit like jet lag; you felt hungry and tired, or not hungry and tired, all at the wrong times.

Susannah began to set out plates and spoons, William sat on the floor and their mother was lifting a heavy iron pot out of the cauldron. Jack went to see what was in it, edging his way round the table and dodging Mrs Roe in the process. He had to duck under a line of washing which steamed and gave off an unpleasant smell like damp dog.

The rain outside and the heat within had made the kitchen fuggy and warm, so that the little window panes were steamed up with condensation. Jack resisted the temptation to write on them; Susannah might get the blame and then she'd fall out with him again. He peeped into the cauldron. Nothing very much; just a round ball of something, tied in a cloth and floating in water.

Suddenly the door from the street was pushed open and Susannah's father came in, dripping wet. He pulled off a long cloak and shook it vigorously.

"Joshua, take care! You will drown us all."

Mr Roe hung his cloak on the hook at the back of the door, and then sat down with the rest of his family. He cleared his throat. "Bless this food to thy use and us to thy service. Amen."

"Hey, we used to say that in the Infants," said Jack, grinning.

Susannah smiled.

They're certainly a religious lot, he thought. I wonder if everybody's like that here?

"Well, Hannah. I have bad news to impart." Mr Roe's forehead was creased in a frown. His wife and daughter looked at him with anxious faces. They paused in the act of picking up their spoons, as if in a game of statues. William sucked enthusiastically on a piece of bread, unconcerned.

"What is it, Joshua?"

"George Viccars is dead. I had the news from Widow Cooper."

"God rest his soul, poor young man."

"Aye, but worse news still. They say . . ."

"Jack, Jack, Jack. Soon, Jack, soon, Jack, soon, Jack. Soon, soon, soon." The cries grew louder. Jack covered his ears, clenched his fists to the side of his head.

"No!"

And then the voices were soft again; crooning, lulling, comforting.

"Soon, soon." The whispers were his own this time. He held his head in his hands and rocked himself backwards and forwards on the stairs. The figures in the kitchen were blurred as though a net curtain had been placed in front of them. They moved in slow motion; sound had been extracted. Through the curtain, Jack saw Susannah, watching him. Open mouthed she gazed at him; fascinated, horrified. Somewhere a door closed: a door with no handle.

Chapter 7
Tom's Betrayal

Jack stirred in his bed, snuggled deeper into the patch of warmth his body had made. He woke slowly and his mind wandered aimlessly for a while. Then he remembered: or rather, didn't remember. Last thing he knew he'd been sitting on the steps listening to Susannah's father saying that someone had died. George somebody or other. Jack mentally shrugged his shoulders. So? So how did I get back? He was sure that he hadn't gone up to the cradle, hadn't turned the acorn. "But I can't be sure of anything these days," he said aloud.

He turned on to his front and pushed his arms under the pillow. He didn't understand how he travelled to Eyam even when he did use the cradle. OK he turned the acorn, but beyond that he didn't have a clue. With or without the cradle; what did it matter?

"Jack." His mother's voice rang up the stairs.

"Breakfast."

Breakfast! You could die in this house and there'd still be breakfast.

He fumbled for his glasses on the bedside table: clock, book, lamp, half-eaten apple, sticky tape: no glasses.

He dropped his legs over the side of the bed and hauled himself up with an effort. He felt heavy and tired, as though he'd put on weight overnight. He groped for his clothes and pulled them on in the dark.

He yawned all the way down the stairs and into the kitchen. "Can't find my glasses."

His father took him by the shoulders and steered him back into the hall and in front of the mirror.

"Oh," said Jack. He was wearing them. "Must have slept in them." He peered closer, took off his glasses and rubbed his eyes. The indentations at the side of his nose were redder and deeper than usual.

"I'm surprised they stayed on," said Mum, sitting down at the table. "The way you heave and groan in bed, I wouldn't have thought they stood a chance."

"I expect I just lay peacefully on my back with my hands clasped together like a saint."

"Well, that's where the resemblance ends," grinned Dad.

"What's this? Jokes before breakfast. Won

the pools, Dad?"

"Can't I make a joke without people wondering if I'm all right?" He wore a mock, pained expression on his face.

"Not before ten o'clock, you can't," said Jack, pulling out a chair.

The unusually bright start to breakfast trailed off and lapsed into silence. Only the chink of knife on plate, the rustling of the newspaper, interrupted it. Jack mulled over his new, secret life. He looked at his parents, preoccupied with their own thoughts, and wondered what they would say if he told them about Eyam. At any moment, he thought, I could completely shatter their peace. I could do something really awful, like going to the local newspaper and telling them everything. The first thing Mum and Dad would know about it would be a reporter knocking on the door.

Jack pondered on the possible results with satisfaction. He'd be famous. People would come from all over the world to interview him. His parents would treat him with a new respect, not think of him as a kid any more. Jack Rutherford, boy wonder from Derby, Tom had said. Jack knew that he'd been joking. But it wasn't a joke; not really. That's how it would be.

"What are you looking so happy about?"

"What?"

"You look like a dog with two tails," said Mum.

"That's a cliché, Mother." They'd been doing clichés at school and now the world seemed riddled with them.

"And where would we be without clichés. That's what I'd like to know."

"We'd have to think of original ways to say things."

"Ha-ha, very funny. Sometimes, Jack Rutherford, you sound almost as pompous as your father." She kissed him on the head.

"I heard that," said Dad, from behind his newspaper.

In the bathroom mirror, Jack experimented with different images for when the TV cameras came. He tried damping his hair down with water, but it still stuck up. He lodged his glasses on different parts of his nose. The further they were towards the end of it, he decided, the more intelligent he looked. He tried different facial expressions: a curled lip here, a raised eyebrow there. "Face it, Rutherford," he told himself with a sigh, "You're no oil painting."

It was all a dream anyway. Jack knew perfectly well that he'd never tell his parents anything, much less the newspapers or television. His glory would have to remain hidden. He hadn't even asked Mum about Eyam, thanks to wretched Alison. Ah well!

Friday morning was Jack's favourite. The whole weekend to look forward to and double English to kick off the day. He sauntered into class with a smile on his face.

Tom was sitting in their usual place. Jack slung his bag on to the table and flopped down beside him. Tom, slowly and deliberately, turned his back and looked out of the window.

"Hey, what's the matter with you? Get out of bed the wrong side?" He flopped down beside his friend. As he did so, he noticed Simon Smith sauntering towards them.

"Morning, me old mate." He was not talking to Jack.

"Hey up, Si." Tom turned to Jack. "Clear off, Rutherford, my friend wants to sit there." He emphasised the word friend.

"But I'm your friend, Tom." Even as he said it, Jack was aware that he sounded wimpish. The kind of person Simon Smith couldn't stand.

Tim forced his face close up to Jack's. "Go away. You're no longer wanted."

He felt a hard knot, like a fist, clench and tighten in his stomach. He groped for his bag and forced his shaking legs across the classroom floor. He had no idea where he was going.

"Hey, watch it." Jane Cooper clutched at her shoulder where Jack, seeing nothing, had collided into her.

"Wrong direction, I'm afraid. You've got an hour and a half of me to put up with before you can escape." Mr Nixon put his hands on Jack's shoulders and turned him around.

Jack drew a deep breath and forced himself back into the classroom. He felt so humiliated by Tom's behaviour that he couldn't believe it had gone unnoticed. Yet it had. Everyone else seemed busy with their own affairs. Only Simon and Tom looked at him. Their sarcastic smiles were so alike that Jack wondered if they'd been practising them especially for him. He looked round for a chair and sidled into one near the back.

"This morning," said Mr Nixon, sitting on the edge of his desk and swinging his legs, "I'd like to talk a little about fantasy, and use our discussion as the basis for a short story. Now, can anybody tell me what we mean by fantasy? Yes, Lisa?"

Misery engulfed Jack. He heard almost nothing of the class discussion, so overwhelmed was he at the thought of not having Tom as a friend. Tom had been around since playgroup days and they'd never fallen out before. He couldn't understand it. What was he supposed to have done? And Simon

Smith of all people. He felt utterly alone.

"Is this lack of attention I see before me, or merely the musings of a creative genius?"

Jack blushed and swallowed. People were looking at him and giggling.

"Er, the musings of a creative genius." He gave himself a mental pat on the back. At least he'd managed to salvage some dignity.

"So glad to hear it. Our theme is fantasy in case you'd forgotten. I await your finished story with anticipation."

Jack looked at the blank paper. Fantasy. He couldn't think of anything. He gazed at the bent heads, looked out of the window, heard the shuffling of paper, the scrape of a chair, the occasional cough. Fantasy. He chewed on his pen. Of course! I'm the only person in this room, he thought, qualified to write about fantasy. I've had my own real fantasy. Stupid; there's no such thing as real fantasy. A thing's either real or fantasy. The things that are happening to me are real, it's just that they'd seem like fantasy to anyone else. Better write something. And as he wrote, he felt the most extraordinary sense of relief, as though putting down a heavy weight he was about to drop.

"Can we stop there, please?"

Jack's head shot up in surprise. He'd been writing for an hour, yet that hour had slipped by without his being aware of it.

"Now I've stopped you a little bit early because I'd like to hear what some of you have written so far. I know most of you haven't finished yet, so that can be your homework. Jack, I'm going to pick on you."

Jack flinched. Normally he enjoyed reading out his work. Writing was something he did well and he took pride in it. But not today. Please not today.

"Come on, Jack."

He stumbled over the first few words. Then his voice lifted and strengthened. His story unfolded again before him; the story of Susannah, William, and an antique cradle. He felt the power of his words enfold his audience, was aware of their absolute silence; there was not the slightest rustle or murmur. The silence continued after he'd finished; people seemed to be in an almost trance-like state. And then Mr Nixon started to clap. Slowly one or two others joined in, until everyone was clapping. Everybody except Tom and Simon Smith. They glared at him as if he'd done something terrible.

"Thanks, Jack. That was marvellous." Mr Nixon was smiling at him.

"D'you think something like that could really happen, Sir?" Tom looked from Mr Nixon to Jack.

"No, I don't. When we talked about the

nature of fantasy, we decided that it usually involved scenes or events which couldn't happen in real life. D'you remember?"

"Well, yes." Tom hesitated, then turned to look at Jack again. "It's just that Jack's told me this story before. He reckons it really happened to him."

As though by some automatic signal, the whole class turned to look at Jack so that his cheeks burned with humiliation. Everyone would think he was mad; no one would believe him; everyone would laugh at him. Why was Tom doing this?

Mr Nixon looked at the two boys. "I suspect that what Jack told you may have been in confidence, Tom. We need to respect one another's confidences."

The boy appeared untouched by the rebuke. He winked at Simon and they bent their heads together in huddled whispers.

Mr Nixon came over to Jack as the rest of the class went to break.

"Having problems?"

Jack nodded.

"That was a superb piece of writing you know. It's a long time since I've heard anything so good. Make sure you finish it."

Jack nodded again.

"And Jack?"

"Yes?"

"If you need to talk, you know where to find me."

"Thanks."

The air outside was sharp as a knife edge. Jack drew in his breath as it seared his face and ears, gasped for breath as his lungs seemed to fill with ice. But the cold seemed to sear his brain too, so that his thoughts became sharper and clearer. The feeling of humiliation condensed into something keener. Anger burst in his veins like a series of sharp explosions. How dare he make me look a fool in front of the entire class? How dare he?

He turned as Tom's voice interrupted.

"Well, if it isn't the old genius himself. Derby's answer to William Shakespeare. Pray let me grovel a little."

Tom bowed low, one arm held across his front, the other clutching a can of coke. "Would you care for a drink, sire?"

"He doesn't want a drink, he wants a shower. He needs his big hot head cooling down, don't you Rutherbum?" Simon pulled the can of coke from Tom's hand and shook it at Jack, so that the dark brown liquid fizzed towards him. Jack ducked and the coke splashed harmlessly onto the ground.

"Hey, that's my coke you're throwing around." Tom pulled the can from Simon's hand. "We don't want our little genius getting dirty, do we? He might get his sticky hands all over that nice new cradle of his."

"Just keep out of my way. I don't know what's the matter with you, but just keep out of my way." Jack's fists were clenching and unclenching. He knew that his voice was shaking with anger and hoped Tom wouldn't think it was fear. "After all the things you've said about Simon Smith, I'm surprised you can bring yourself to go anywhere near him. You're a hypocrite."

Jack saw the two of them glance at each other and then quickly away again. Simon looked offended, but Tom tried to bluster his way out of this embarrassment.

"A hypo-what? A hippopotamus? Looks like he's swallowed a dictionary again, Si." Tom took a swig of coke.

"Well, he *is* Derby's answer to William Shakespeare." Simon rubbed his hands together and blew on them for warmth. He obviously wasn't going to let a small hiccup like this spoil his new friendship.

Jack pushed past him and headed towards the door. Tom clutched at his shoulder and pulled him back, but Jack shrugged him off.

"Just a little word in your ear, me old mate. You're either mad or a liar. Choose which."

Jack pushed at the door and stumbled along the corridor to the cloakroom. He hid himself in a corner.

Mad! Was he mad? Was he? He hadn't thought of that. He'd not thought that there might be something wrong with him. Mad! No! No, I'm not mad! But then, would I know if I was? Do mad people know that they're mad? This was even more scary. If there's no way of knowing if you're mad, then how can you be sure that you're not? He breathed out heavily. He remembered Susannah's fear of being thought mad, and her even greater fear of being thought a witch. The thought of Susannah comforted him. She would understand just how he felt.

The bell was ringing for the end of break and a crowd of panting, red-faced boys surged into the cloakroom. They brought the cold air in with them and Jack shivered as he stood up.

On the way to art, he found that someone had fallen into stride with him. He glanced sideways: David Clarke, Simon Smith's ex best mate; he of the snowball fight.

"You OK?"

"Yeah, yeah," Jack lied.

"Is it true, what Tom said in English? Did you really tell him those things happened to you?"

"No," he lied again.

"Well, according to Tom you did. He's told everybody."

Jack said nothing. He felt sick. Tom had betrayed him, there was no other word for it. He'd never trust him again as long as he lived.

"Anyway if you ask me," David continued, "They deserve each other."

"Who?"

"Tom and Simon, of course."

"Not half," said Jack.

"Brilliant story though. Wish I'd written it." David grinned.

"Thanks," said Jack.

Jack was half watching a nature programme, when he realised that he'd meant to go to the library. He'd been so wrapped in gloom, he supposed, that he hadn't given it so much as a passing thought. In his mind, he'd gone over and over the scenes with Tom. He couldn't stop thinking about it, couldn't leave it alone. Each action replay deepened the gloom. But it didn't stop him rewinding the tape.

He felt tired. With his hand on the cradle, he debated whether he should give Eyam a miss tonight. He was so tired. No, no, he'd go. He didn't have to stay long. Just a quick hello.

Chapter 8
In Widow Cooper's Cottage

Jack pulled himself to his feet and looked out of the bedroom window. It was raining, just as it had been when he'd left. It came in great, slanting sheets that turned the surface of the street into bubbling chocolate: at least that's what it looked like. He turned at the sound of Susannah's voice.

"Are you recovered, Jack?"

"What from?"

"You acted most strangely just now." The girl tutted at Jack's blank expression. "When Father told us of George Viccars' death."

"Just now?" He looked even more puzzled.

"A few moments since. What ails you, boy?"

"I've been home since then. It's a whole day."

Susannah stared at him silently. "Indeed, boy." She looked at him still; looked deeply and hard. "I do not understand your doings,

Jack."

"Me neither." Two minutes equals three days, he told himself. Except that sometimes it does and sometimes it doesn't because the rules keep changing. Eyam time. It doesn't make sense. He shrugged his shoulders.

"I am going with Mother to see Widow Cooper." Her voice was brisk and businesslike. "There is much to be done now that Mr Viccars is dead, and Mother thinks I shall be a comfort to her." She flounced importantly to the door.

"Why are you going? It's not as if you're a grown woman or anything." He remembered his Gran's funeral. He'd been kept firmly out of the way. Nobody had actually said that death was nothing to do with children, but they might as well have done because that's what they meant.

"That is of no account. We must all help our neighbours, young and old alike. It is God's will."

Does she really believe in God as much as all that, he wondered? But then everyone in Eyam seemed to talk about God as if he lived there; like one of the neighbours.

"Let me come with you then."

"If you wish."

Widow Cooper lived at the other end of the street, beyond the church. By the time they arrived, Jack's trainers were squelching in filthy mud.

He saw a worried face appear briefly at a window at the sound of their knocking. Widow Cooper was a tiny, frail-looking woman who shivered beneath the folds of a great shawl. She had wiry grey hair; like a used brillo pad, he thought.

He wondered if his footprints would be invisible, and remembered the imprint he'd made in the mud by the water trough. Had anyone else seen it, though? He took his trainers off, just in case. He didn't want Mrs Roe going on about demons again.

"I am so sorry, my dear." Mrs Roe unwrapped William from her cloak and gave him to Susannah. Then she folded the little woman in her arms.

"He was such a good, quiet man to be taken so sudden." Widow Cooper wiped her face on the edge of her shawl. "Would you like to see him?"

Jack started to laugh. Fancy going to look at a dead body. He could just imagine them standing round the bed, and George Viccars saying, Excuse me if I don't get up. Susannah looked at him sternly and he felt ashamed of himself. But the more she looked, the more he laughed. He didn't know why; it wasn't funny. The tears rolled down his face and misted up his glasses. His sides ached and he wanted to stop. But he couldn't.

Susannah glared at him once more, and then followed the others upstairs to pay her last respects to George Viccars.

As soon as they moved away, he saw that there was a boy in the room, older than himself. He sat with his hands clasped together, looking into the fire.

"And Edward stayed off work to keep me company, bless his soul." Widow Cooper panted back downstairs, followed by Susannah and Mrs Roe, in procession.

Some company, thought Jack.

"Good day, Edward." Susannah smiled and wriggled her shoulders at the boy. Edward blushed and muttered into the fire.

"Stupid girl," Jack muttered.

The visitors sat in an oak settle and Susannah gazed at Edward across the hearth.

"He'd just received some bales of cloth from London, my dear. He was that pleased. He could get on with his orders, he said. He was doing very well for himself, my dear. I was proud to have him lodge with me."

Widow Cooper broke some bread into two wooden bowls set on the table, and then poured a foul-smelling milky concoction over the top. Jack watched the dark bread swell as it absorbed the liquid.

"Are you certain you will not take some,

Hannah?"

"No, I thank you, Mary."

"The cloth was a bit damp," she continued, "so George put it in front of the fire to dry. A terrible stench there was with it. And the fleas! You should have seen the fleas." Widow Cooper shook her head. "I fear they may not all be gone now." She slurped at the soggy mess in front of her. "Then he took the fever."

Jack squirmed on the hard wooden bench and scratched at his arms and neck. Fleas, ugh!

He noticed Edward Cooper smiling at Susannah, who looked at the floor, demurely.

He went and stood in front of Edward so that Susannah couldn't see the boy. She scowled ferociously and Jack grinned.

"You like Susannah, do you?" Jack flicked at Edward's hair. "Want to marry her, do you?" The boy lifted his hand and slapped at the side of his head.

Susannah looked as if she wanted to murder Jack. Her face burned in bright embarrassment.

"Well, I wouldn't bother, if I were you. She's a bad tempered old trout. And she smells."

Susannah nearly fell off the settle at this. She hurried to the window and looked out, trying to hide her blushes. Jack stood next to her, holding his nose.

"Don't worry, Susannah, everybody's smelly in Eyam. It's a really smelly place. No offence."

"I would strike you if my Mother were not here," she said, under her breath.

"Now, now, young lady. No talking to yourself." Jack marched back to his bench with a smirk on his face. Widow Cooper was still talking.

"And Joshua has the making of the coffin in hand, so there is nought else to be done for the present."

Mrs Roe heaved herself from the settle. "I will send Susannah in the morning. She is a good girl and will be a help to you." Susannah smiled. "But now we must wend our way."

The rain had changed to a silken drizzle. The church bell boomed, solemnly. Jack had given up all hope of saving his footwear. The mud had oozed through to his feet and every step produced a slurping, sucking noise as he struggled to keep his trainers on.

"I am glad your feet are in a mess," Susannah hissed, "I hope they drop off."

"I said I was sorry." He felt a bit guilty now; he knew he'd been horrible to her. But there was no need for her to keep going on about it, was there?

Later, when his feet were dry, he felt better. He watched Mrs Roe pour broth into an earthenware jug and place it in a cloth bag packed with straw.

Susannah came rushing down the stairs,

pulling her skirt up at both sides, so that she didn't trip.

"One day, Susannah Roe, you will find yourself at the bottom of those stairs with your neck broken." Her mother held out the wrapped jug. "Will you take this to your father?"

"He's a carpenter," Susannah explained. "And the finest in the Peak, some say. That is why we have such fine furniture in our house."

"Are you rich, then?"

"I never thought of it before. But no, not rich, like the folk at the Hall, and not poor, like the farm labourers. But Father sometimes works in grand houses and copies their ways. He first saw the like of William's cradle at Bradshaw Hall."

The lane curled steeply to the left and they came to a low building with a thatched roof. Susannah lifted the latch and the door scraped over a bumpy earth floor.

Jack stepped into the warmth of the carpenter's shop. He breathed in the warm air, scented with the sweet, sharp smell of newly planed wood. The floor was covered with creamy curls and shavings and the wall was hung with an assortment of heavy black tools.

Susannah's father stood behind a workbench, and wore a leather jerkin over a rough, colourless shirt. He held a large piece of pale wood in his hands, which he lowered gently onto a coffin on the workbench.

"Hello, my dear." He smiled at Susannah and gestured at the coffin. "What do you think?"

The girl ran her hands over the wood, stroking it as though it were a piece of velvet. Jack watched her and wondered why she was not afraid of it, as he was.

"It is fine, Father. George Viccars would not have been ashamed of it."

"Aye. I reckon you're right, my girl." Mr Roe looked at the coffin with pride.

Susannah unpacked the jug of soup from the cloth bag and put it on the floor.

"Thank you, child."

"Mother says you must not take a chill, with hot sun one minute and rain the next. The broth will help." She poured the liquid into a goblet. "Drink up, Father."

"Yes, Mistress Roe." He bowed low, and they laughed together.

"Can we go?" said Jack loudly. "It gives me the creeps in here with all these coffins."

"There is only one coffin." Susannah closed the door behind them. "And why you should dislike it so, I cannot imagine. It is a beautiful coffin."

"Because of dead people," said Jack, as if this

explained everything.

"In the midst of life, we are in death," quoted Susannah.

"Oh, we *are* cheerful, Little Miss Sunday School."

"It is but the truth," she said smugly.

"Is it from the bible?" He thought this might improve his image.

"Indeed, I think I have mentioned it before, Jack, that you are a very strange boy."

"Once or twice," said Jack.

"You should not be so afraid, boy. Death is not the end. It is a new beginning."

"Me? Afraid? Huh!" Jack hit at a hedge with a stick he'd just found, so that raindrops splashed out at them.

Susannah tutted and shook her cloak. "You are just like a boy, Jack Rutherford."

"So I am." He wanted to provoke her; poke at her smugness with some clever words. Get his own back for once.

"Of course in my time you're already dead. You died years ago."

Susannah stopped and looked at him over her shoulder. She said nothing; just turned and walked on again.

Jack beat the hedge even harder, with a big grin on his face. That'd give her something to think about.

"And you," she said softly, so that he had to

catch up with her to hear, "have not yet been born. Which may explain one or two things." She marched on, her head held high and with a smile of satisfaction on her face.

Jack blinked and straightened his glasses. Does anybody ever get the better of the girl? He drew numbers in the air with his finger. Susannah Roe – 10. Jack Rutherford – 3. He heard an imaginary crowd, clapping and cheering, and saw, in his mind's eye, Susannah bowing as flowers were thrown at her feet. Jack Rutherford, the also ran, stared dismally from behind a tattered curtain.

He began to whistle and lengthened his stride to overtake her. He was going home. It was way past his bedtime.

The minute Jack woke on Saturday morning he had the feeling that something awful had happened. Then he remembered, Tom had fallen out with him. There were other people he could hang around with if he wanted to, but they weren't real friends like Tom. Like Tom used to be, that is.

He sat up. The best thing was to get on with something, not to mope and gloom all over the place. He would go to the library straight after breakfast. Jack ran up the steps, pushed open the heavy glass doors, and looked up at the domed roof with the small gallery running round it. It was the first thing he always did on entering the library. Ever since he'd first come here as a small boy he'd loved the painted ceiling with its names of writers in gold lettering: Dickens, Goldsmith, Fielding. Busts of the famous peered over the edge of the gallery. He used to think they watched him.

He made for the information desk.

"Yes, we've got something on Eyam. It's quite a popular topic in schools. You want the local history section."

Jack followed her, his eyes transfixed by the mass of hairgrips criss-crossing the back of her thin, brown hair. One of them was hanging loose and he fought the desire to pull it out.

"Is it for a school project?" She handed him a thin booklet and smiled encouragingly.

"No, it's for interest."

"That's what I like to see: interest."

A project? Why should anyone want to do a project on Eyam? He pulled out a chair, sat down and started to leaf through the pages. It looked pretty boring. Geology, agriculture, customs, well-dressing, lead mining, plague. He began to read.

The summer of 1665 was one of drought, owing to the long, hot summer. The wakes, held in August, were well attended because of the fine weather. People thronged from the outlying villages to join in the celebrations.

The wakes! Jack cast his mind back; saw again the colour, smelled the smells, relived the events of that hot day.

Jack thought it odd that the writer should choose the very time that he had been there. He could have written about any period of the village's history, yet he'd chosen August, 1665. It was really peculiar.

Then, quite clearly, he understood the importance of what he was reading. He, Jack Rutherford, had been present at an event which had happened more than three hundred years ago. An event, as Mr Nixon would say, in recorded history.

He'd been there and he wanted to tell the world! Look, Mr Nixon, Tom, Mum, Joe Bloggs, I was there, actually there! I saw it all! He looked round at the other readers. They weren't at all impressed. He read on.

But in September, things were to change. George Viccars, a travelling tailor, died of bubonic plague. He was lodging with a widow, Mary Cooper, and her two sons, Jonathan and Edward, when he received a box of cloth from London. It is believed that this cloth harboured the plague-carrying fleas. The death of George Viccars was the first of many. Two hundred and fifty-nine people are believed to have died of the plague, out of a population of around three hundred and fifty.

He put the book down slowly. Two hundred and fifty nine people! Two hundred and fifty-nine people in that small village had died of the plague. What about Susannah? And William? Jack picked up the booklet, ran between the bookcases, and almost flung it at the atonished librarian.

He wanted to run. He wanted to run so fast that it would all go away. So that the memory of what he had just read would be blown from his brain by the force of his speed.

But he could not blow it away. He saw, as he sped home, that it was impossible. Once you know something as enormous as this, he realised, then you know it for ever, whether you choose to or not. There is no choice.

It had all happened so long ago. Susannah and William were dead anyway. Hadn't he taunted Susannah with the fact? But when did they die? When? Did they die of the plague? If they did, then there was no question of his ever going back there again; he couldn't bear it.

As Jack put his hand on the back door, he had an overwhelming desire to be tucked up in bed, warm and safe. He wanted his mother to read to him like she used to do; read him stories with happy endings. He would be safe. He would fall asleep, and when he woke up in the morning everything would be all right. But as he pushed his way into the kitchen he knew that it would not. It wasn't that simple.

Chapter 9
The Funeral

Jack didn't go to Eyam that night; the first night since the cradle's arrival that he hadn't done so. He longed to go back, and yet he was scared of what he might find there.

On Saturday afternoon he had gone to the library again and copied out passages from the Eyam booklet. He read and reread the same few words until he knew them by heart.

Tom hadn't phoned or called round. Jack wasn't surprised; just fed up. Mum was tired and spent both afternoons in bed so that Jack had felt abandoned in the empty house. Not that it was really empty, but Dad had been irritable and they'd both crept around so that they wouldn't disturb Mum. Sheets of brown rain had driven the snow away. If Jack had been able to paint a picture of that weekend, it would have been just smudges of dark brown, edged in black. By Sunday evening he could no longer bear his own company. He would return to Eyam.

The clock had just chimed eleven and the house was quiet. Dad was on call and had left to see a patient. Mum was asleep.

He felt like a small boy again, with an anticipation so keen that he wanted to jump up and down in excitement. It seemed so long since he'd seen them all, and he'd been so miserable. He couldn't wait to be there again. He turned the acorn.

It was the quietest journey so far with only a gentle rolling sensation to mark its passing. There were no voices, no whispers. The silence seemed like a reproach.

The house was quiet. Jack listened. It was so still he could almost feel it. And then he heard the bell. The deep tones rang clearly into the stillness, like a slow march.

He went to the head of the stairs and listened; nothing. There was no one in the kitchen. He poked his head round the open parlour door; not a soul.

The street was empty too. The cottage doors were like blank faces turned towards him. The sky was leaden and the air damp, but at least the rain had stopped.

Jack shivered. Where on earth was everybody? He trudged slowly up the muddy lane, his hands in his pockets. The place was deserted; it was uncanny.

The sound of the bell grew louder. And then, as he rounded a bend in the street, he saw a procession of people coming towards him. At the head of it was a group of men, supporting a coffin on their shoulders. They turned into the churchyard and walked slowly, solemnly, towards the porch.

They were met by Parson Mompesson, whose voice rose and fell in harmony with the sonorous booming of the church bell. "I am the resurrection and the life saith the Lord: he that believeth in me, though he were dead, yet shall he live . . ."

Jack darted forward, not wanting to miss anything. He watched the long, winding line of people shuffling and rolling towards the church while Mompesson's intonation continued. ". . . and whosoever liveth and believeth in me shall never die."

Behind the coffin came Widow Cooper, holding onto the arm of a young man who looked remarkably like Edward. But there was no sign of Edward.

Jack thought how strange it was, that he should arrive in Eyam just in time to see George Viccars' funeral.

He leaned against the trunk of a yew tree, half-hidden by its low branches, and scanned the procession for Susannah. He spotted her towards the end of it, with her parents and William. She looked sad. The whole village looked sad. He followed her down the path and tapped her on the shoulder as she entered the church. She jumped violently.

"Jack!" Susannah glanced nervously over her shoulder but no one had heard.

"Chack." William waved his arm over his mother's shoulder.

"How come there are so many people here?" Jack saw that every pew was filled and people were moving along to make room for others.

Susannah couldn't reply now that they were inside the church. She clasped her hands under her chin and looked thoroughly miserable. Strange really, thought Jack; I didn't think she knew George Viccars very well.

Parson Mompesson stood up in the pulpit, looking like a black eagle about to swoop. He wasn't tall though. Funny that, Jack looked around the church, nobody was. It was something he'd noticed at the wakes: how small everyone seemed.

He caught Susannah's eye and she smiled at him; a funny sort of smile, twisted between the words of the hymn she was singing. He smiled back and felt remarkably happy considering he was at a funeral. He'd never been to a funeral before, but at the moment anything was better than life in Derby.

"Jack." He froze at the sound of the whisper. The blood rushed to his head so that he thought he was going to faint. "Jack." It came again; gentle, reproachful. How could you have forgotten? it seemed to say. He felt himself sway. He put out a hand to save himself and heard the click of a closing door. He saw the door swirling away from him inside his head; the door with no handle.

He had almost forgotten; he had almost forgotten that this was the beginning of it all. A small book, in a library far away in time, did not seem to have much to do with *this* village, *this* time. In the happiness of being here, he had forgotten the dreadful words he had read in the library.

Mompesson was speaking. His voice boomed into the silent church and echoed off the walls.

" . . . And our dear brother, Edward Cooper, who was loved by all of us, as a quiet, Christian soul . . ."

Jack heard no more. He looked at Susannah, his mouth open in shock. "But I thought this was George Viccars' funeral." His voice was too loud; an intrusion in the quiet church.

"Edward Cooper's dead?"

Susannah nodded. She put her finger on her lip for Jack to be quiet.

George Viccars, Widow Cooper, Edward

117

Cooper. The names filled his head with the weight of their importance. It was happening again. In some strange turnabout of time, the events of Eyam were being replayed: slowly, irrevocably, as though on some eternal treadmill.

He watched the people listening intently to Parson Mompesson's words. It was happening all over again and they did not know. One thing was for certain: he was not going to tell them, even if that were possible. What would be the point?

He trooped out beside Susannah and followed the coffin round to the side of the church.. A slight wind had risen and the branches of the yew trees were bowing gently, politely. An invisible wave rippled across the grass. I'm like the wind, he thought. I can make things move without anyone seeing me.

He dodged through the crowd standing around the graveside. Folk were pulling cloaks tight around their shoulders for the day was growing colder.

"In the midst of life we are in death . . ." Jack looked up and found Susannah watching him. D'you remember? her eyes asked him. Yes, he did remember; and he wondered how many funerals she had been to, that she should know the words by heart.

". . . earth to earth, ashes to ashes, dust to

dust . . ."

And I know those words, thought Jack. But only because I've heard them on the telly. He watched, fascinated, as Widow Cooper bent to pick up a handful of earth. He heard it spatter on the coffin. Poor Edward Cooper, gone to dust.

People started to move away from the graveside, alone or in groups. Jack tapped at Susannah's arm.

"How did he die?" He knew the answer of course; he just hoped that he was wrong; that by some miracle history would not repeat itself.

"They say it was the plague."

"Oh." Stupid really; he shouldn't have asked.

"Some of us are going back to Widow Cooper's to keep her company. Mother sat up all night with the body and is weary, so she will not come."

"Sat with the body?"

"Yes. Widow Cooper needed a woman's company."

"Weird, weird, weird," said Jack, shaking his head.

"He had the plague tokens, you see. Red rings all over his chest. Poor Edward." Widow Cooper sucked at her lips, just like his mother when she was blotting lipstick.

Jack lounged against a sideboard and watched the small group of people who had returned to the cottage. A boy, the one who looked so like Edward, handed out the ale that Widow Cooper poured from a large jug.

"Now my fear is for Jonathan." The widow blew her nose and people nodded and murmured in sympathy.

"No, Mother. You must not fear for me. I am stronger than my brother. Edward's spirit was weak and that is why he succumbed." The boy, Jonathan Cooper, reached up his hand and grasped the high mantelpiece, leaning sideways against it.

Out of the corner of his eye, Jack saw something black, flick past the window and disappear. There was a gentle knocking at the door.

Widow Cooper scampered across the kitchen and peered through the window. "'Tis the parson." She straightened her bonnet and pulled her shawl tighter before opening the door. "Reverend Mompesson. It is kind of you to come again so soon."

The parson stooped through the doorway. He swept off his hat and cloak and handed them to the widow.

"Sit you down, Parson. Sit you down." A small, elderly man, shuffled from his seat.

Mompesson nodded his thanks and sat in

the proffered chair, crossing his long, black legs as he did so.

The elderly man stood behind him with both hands on the back of the chair, like a bodyguard.

"Mistress Cooper, the words I have for you are hard. But I beg that you, and all here present, listen carefully." He leaned forward and looked from face to face. "We can hide from the fact no longer: Edward and George Viccars died from the plague. In the pursuance of his trade, George Viccars ordered a box of cloth from London. I believe that this is how the plague came to our village. That cloth must now be burned, along with all of the victim's clothing. We must take no risks. The pestilence may yet survive in the cloth."

There was an outbreak of murmuring. Heads bent together in whispered consultations.

"And I fear it is unwise to gather so close together. From now on we must keep our distance from afflicted households, unless it is to offer help, as the Lord would have us do."

No one looked at Mompesson. He turned, and it seemed to Jack that the parson looked straight at him: a penetrating ice-blue stare that made the boy stop his lounging and stand up straight. He shivered and looked away. The parson had not seen him, yet had seemed to know what he was thinking.

He looked at Susannah, and saw that she had noticed his squirming. Trust her not to miss anything.

Mompesson drew his gaze away as Widow Cooper spoke to him. She spoke haltingly, as if summoning the courage to speak the words.

"'Tis a crying shame to burn good clothes. There are poor enough in this parish to be glad of such apparel."

"But they would not be glad of the plague. I beg you to burn the clothes at once. No more lives must be lost." Mompesson looked at the small gathering of people. "Who will help me undertake this task?"

No one spoke. No one met Mompesson's eyes. Folk looked at the floor, out of the window, into the fire; anywhere but at the parson. At last, a young woman spoke.

"I think we must trust the Reverend. If he says the plague may survive in the cloth, then I believe him. I will help you, Sir."

"Aye, Aye, she is right. Let the job be done quickly." The elderly man patted the back of Mompesson's chair, as if to seal the decision.

Jack felt as if he were watching a film. He felt like an observer, as someone who has no part to play in the events around him. No one could see him. He may as well not have been there.

"You are very kind, Reverend. You are all kind." Widow Cooper included all in her glance. "But it does seem a pitiful waste. I do not understand how anyone should be taken sick from a dead man's apparel."

Mompesson nodded. "I confess that I myself do not fully understand how it is so. But it is said to be possible and we must take every precaution."

"Then I will sort the clothes now. Susannah, will you come with me?" The widow held out her hand to the girl.

"No, Susannah! Don't!" Jack ran after her and pulled at her shoulder. The girl shrugged him off.

"Don't you understand, you stupid girl?" Jack bounded up the stairs after her. Fear and anger shot from every pore of his skin. Fear and anger; they had become so mixed up that he didn't know which was which. "You might catch the plague. You might die!"

She reached out and touched his shoulder; looked into his eyes. In that moment she seemed no longer a girl but someone very wise; someone who understood a great deal more than Jack did.

"I am in God's care, boy. Yet you seem not to understand." She turned and walked slowly up the stairs.

He watched her turn into the bedroom and disappear. These people seemed to know something he did not; he felt foolish and ignorant beside them. Yet he was the one who knew. He was the one who could have told them. Their faith deceived them! They were wrong! Weren't they? He struggled to hold down the fear that threatened to rise and engulf him. Susannah might die.

Back in the cottage bedroom, Jack put his hand on the little acorn. He felt as though there was a tap, somewhere in his body, and all his energy was draining slowly from it. He wanted to go home; he needed to go home. But the acorn wouldn't move.

He tried again; nothing: no blackness, no whispering, no falling; nothing. He screamed inwardly: Let me out of here! But the acorn refused to budge. Jack swallowed hard. He was trapped. He might never get home again.

Chapter 10
In the Dead of Night

"Susannah! Susannah!" Jack hurled himself down the stairs, his feet barely touching the stone treads.

"The acorn's stuck. I can't get back." He could feel himself shaking. His heart seemed to thump its way into his throat and tear the breath away.

Susannah beckoned him into the parlour. "Father mended it while we were at Widow Cooper's. Mother has been asking him for weeks." She put her hand to her chin and frowned. "I never thought of your comings and goings."

"Well, we'll have to unmend it, won't we? It's my flippin' cradle!" He knew that it wasn't; not when he was in Eyam at any rate. But he was being battered by that strange mixture of fear and anger again and he couldn't think straight.

The girl closed the parlour door and rounded on him angrily. "Perhaps the cradle is yours when you are gone from here; I do not know. But I do know that this is William's new-made crib and has been here constantly." She stood with her hand on the door knob, her face flushed. "And it was made by my own Father's hands."

"I know, I know, I'm sorry." He moved to the window and looked out at the narrow street. He didn't want to stay here forever, no matter how much he liked the place.

"The cradle's my way of getting home; I'm stuck without it."

Susannah traced the outline of a flagstone with her foot and stared hard at the floor. "I know!" She looked at Jack and danced enthusiastically towards him. "It is Father's night for the watch and ward."

"What's that?"

"It is the guarding of the village during the hours of darkness. Tonight it is Father's turn. Father and Mr Morten. Do you not have watch and ward in Derby?"

"Well, we might have done in 1665 for all I know; but not now."

"It may be, since Father is out, that I am able to borrow one of his tools and put the crib to rights."

Jack wiped his nose on his sleeve. "D'you

think you can do it?"

"Of course, boy. Do not fret so."

Some of her confidence flowed into him and he felt more cheerful: he'd get back all right.

In the kitchen, Mrs Roe thumped bread dough and hummed. William had a little piece for himself and sat on the table opening and closing his fist so that it oozed through his fingers.

"Chack," he said to his mother, as Jack came through the door.

"Yes, Chack," she smiled. "I cannot think what this Chack word is, Susannah. Can you?"

"No, Mother." She grinned at Jack.

William offered him a piece of grubby dough. "Chack," he said. Jack took the little boy's hand and shook it solemnly. The dough looked almost tempting.

"I'm starving. Is there anything to eat?"

Susannah shrugged her shoulders.

Mrs Roe put the bread into a brick oven at the side of the fireplace. Jack watched, and imagined it coming out again, crisp and brown. He imagined yellow butter, oozing into its grainy warmth. He felt it melt deliciously on to his tongue. He groaned.

"I will find you something later," Susannah whispered.

At supper time, he sat on the stairs and watched. It was torture. Mrs Roe had remained obstinately in the kitchen, so he hadn't eaten. His stomach rumbled noisily.

"I'm starving!" he shouted crossly.

He came and perched on the end of the bench, next to Susannah. It creaked as he sat down.

"Give us a bit," he said.

The girl picked up a piece of bread and wafted it in front of his face. She bit into it and chewed elaborately, staring at Jack as she did so. He pulled a face at her.

"Greedy pig."

He knelt on the floor with his hands outstretched, like a beggar boy.

"Mr and Mrs Roe, parents of this hideous girl, can you not spare a morsel of your fine repast for a poor, starving boy?"

They munched silently. Susannah bent her head and giggled.

"William, have you got any of that dirty bread dough left?"

"Chack," he replied.

"Is that all you can say?"

William smiled sweetly.

It was then that he remembered Mum and Dad. Their faces seemed to float, unbidden, in front of him. He'd tried not to think about them because it made him panic. Usually, he thought, no time passes while I'm here. But supposing things have changed? Supposing it's ages since they saw me? They'll think I've gone missing from my bed. They'll be looking for me. And how can I let them know I'm safe except by getting back again? And I can't get back. I'm stuck. He looked at William who gazed steadily back at him. Jack's eyes filled with tears. He lowered his head on to his arms and felt the tears soak into his jumper. He began to sob.

"Chack," said William. "Chack cry. Poor Chack. Poor boy."

Susannah said nothing. How could she?

Supper continued. Through his sobs, Jack heard the thud of a heavy jug on the table, heard someone scraping a plate with a spoon. He heard Mr Roe's murmured grace and the benches scraping on the flagstones as they were pushed away from the table.

He wiped his runny nose on his sleeve. His face felt hot and swollen and his head ached. He looked at the wet patch on the table, where his tears had fallen. He rubbed it dry with his sleeve and hoped no one had seen it.

Susannah looked at him, her face concerned. He looked away, embarrassed. She put her hand on his shoulder and patted it. "Do not fret, boy."

William had been put to bed and the rest of the family was in the parlour.

Jack sat on a hard wooden chair and stared morosely out of the window at the gathering dusk. Why couldn't they all just go to bed so that he and Susannah could sort things out?

Dusk deepened and blurred the outlines of figures and furniture. Light faded from the room and colour drained away. Jack fidgeted.

Mr Roe read from an enormous bible and sat by the window to catch the last of the daylight. His voice droned monotonously and Jack felt his eyes begin to close. He forced them open again and sat up straight. He stared at the carving on the bible box and followed its intricate curves with his eyes. He murmured his own desperate prayer: Please God, let it work. Please let the acorn turn again. Let me go home. He lifted his head and saw the ever-watchful Susannah, watching him.

He realised that it was dark now, and wondered how it was that he could never pinpoint the exact moment when dusk became dark.

It was time for Mr Roe to go on watch and ward, or whatever it was called.

"May God keep you safe, Joshua."

"Aye, and pray that I shall have no need of this."

He picked up a long wooden pole with an axe at the end which Jack rather liked the look of.

"I wouldn't fancy meeting him on a dark night with that little weapon. Wouldn't mind having a hold of it though."

A fire glowed still in the hearth and the kitchen was transformed into a shadow-filled, flickering cavern. Mrs Roe hadn't noticed that there were three figures silhouetted against the walls. Perhaps his shadow was invisible too.

The woman rolled back the lid from a metal box filled with candles, poked a twig into the fire, and lit the candle from its flame.

Without a word, Susannah took the candle from her and pushed it into a metal holder. It's like watching a silent movie, thought Jack, as he followed them upstairs.

He perched on the end of Susannah's bed. The darkness of the roof space seemed to go on for ever, and he could hear rustling in the thatch. He looked up apprehensively.

"It's only mice," Susannah whispered cheerfully.

"When are you going to get me something to eat?"

"We must stay here till Mother is asleep. She has ears like a dog and will hear us else."

"How long will that be?" If he had to go without food for just five more minutes he would die: he was sure of it.

"She sleeps quickly and sound. You will know from the thunder she makes."

Susannah bent down and scrabbled under the bed. "I almost forgot." She patted her hands over the floorboards. "You left your candle."

Candle? He hadn't got a candle.

The girl's dark shape reappeared. She pushed something heavy and cold into Jack's hand.

"My torch! I'd forgotten all about it." Candle!

He flicked it on and its strong beam filled the room. He shone it into the rafters, from where the rustling seemed to be coming.

"I can't see anything."

"It is a mouse, boy. No more, no less. Did you think it was a bear come to eat you?"

"Where's the loo?" he asked, changing the subject.

"Loo?"

"Toilet. Lavatory. WC." He used every word he could think of. "You know, the place where you have a wee."

"Do you wish to relieve yourself?"

"Yes, I wish to relieve myself," he mimicked. "And I want something to eat and drink, and I want to go home."

"Listen." Susannah laid a hand on his arm. "Mother is asleep."

Snores vibrated from the next room.

"I told you she makes thunder."

They crept downstairs. Susannah fetched

bread and cheese from the dresser and poured water into a goblet.

"I need to go to the loo first. Where is it?"

"You may relieve yourself at the bottom of the garden."

The bottom of the garden? It was worse then camping.

Susannah led the way, holding the torch and playing its beam from side to side. The moon was a brilliant white and gave quite enough light to see by. But Susannah was enjoying herself.

A vegetable garden gave way to a stone wall. Beyond this lay an orchard. The trees were heavy with apples and Jack pulled one off and bit into it. It was sweet and juicy and the best thing he had ever tasted. He reached for another.

Susannah pointed out a low wall with a trench behind it.

"Is this it?"

"Indeed. I shall leave you." She headed off, carrying the torch proudly.

"What am I supposed to wipe my bum with?"

"Are there not mosses and leaves enough for you, boy?"

"Oh, what a silly boy I am," he sang. He found a clump of dock leaves and picked two of the biggest. Who needed toilet paper?

In the kitchen, firelight glinted on the pewter goblet as Jack lifted it to drink. The water was cold and delicious, the bread hard and bitter.

Susannah sat in the hearth like Polly Flinders and shone the torch around the kitchen. "It is far, far better than a candle for you can tell it where to shine. And it does not burn. How strange."

Afterwards, he tried to put things away, but Susannah wouldn't let him. "If things are not where they belong, then Mother will wonder what has been happening."

There wasn't much anyway. The cupboards at home were full of tins and packets of food. It was so easy to go to the fridge and help yourself to yoghurt or lemonade. But here there was so little.

"What you've never had, you never miss," his grandmother was fond of saying. Jack supposed it must be true.

"Now, Jack, we must try and get you home." She lifted a bunch of keys, like a gaoler's, from a hook on the back of the door. Quietly, carefully, she closed the heavy door behind them. As they stepped into the night air Jack felt suddenly free, as if he'd been kept prisoner for weeks and weeks, and had only just been allowed out.

They walked up the hill, past cottages in darkness. Here and there candles flickered, and Jack caught glimpses of faces, polished by firelight. Everywhere was deserted and silent.

"This isn't the way to your father's workshop?" He had so enjoyed their nocturnal prowl that it hadn't occurred to him until now.

"I wondered when you would notice. I wanted to come to church first, to pray for your safe return."

"Well, you don't have to go to church to pray. You can pray anywhere, can't you?"

"But we are here now." She put her hand on Jack's arm. "Let us go in and pray for your return home."

"Can't we pray here?" He didn't fancy the idea of going into a deserted churchyard at night.

"It will be better in church. We will not be discovered at this hour. You are not afraid, are you?"

"No, course I'm not," he lied.

The torchlight lurched and danced down the path to the church door, lighting up a patch of grass here, a gravestone there. The sloping roof of the church looked almost white in the moonlight, and puffs of cloud moved swiftly across the sky. Jack shivered.

The door groaned and creaked as they pushed it open and entered the cold church. A beam of moonlight seared the darkness, piercing the central aisle and disappearing into the pews on the far side of the building.

Susannah reached for his hand and led him slowly, carefully down the aisle towards the altar. At any other time he would have felt stupid and pulled his hand away at once, but now he was scared and her fingers were warm and reassuring.

"What do we have to go all the way down here for?"

"I want to pray at the altar."

She knelt at the rail and Jack knelt beside her.

"What if the parson comes?" His whispers echoed in the cavernous space.

"He will not. If he does we shall hide. How will he see us? Has he eyes of fire, that he can see in the dark?"

More like ice, thought Jack, remembering the parson's stare.

Susannah put her hands together in prayer, the tips of her fingers touching her chin, the white bonnet framing her face and the collar falling in two deep points, almost to her waist. She was marble still; a tombstone effigy.

Jack was too edgy to pray. He looked nervously around him. Across the floor of the aisle, the moonlight polished the metal grating with its milky beam. He saw dark shapes, and a blacker dark so deep no shadow could penetrate. He felt that someone watched him, as though something with tiny feet pattered up and down his spine. He heard the rustle and sigh of leaves tapping at a window. Soon the door would creak open. The shadow of a man would be outlined in the doorway, would walk slowly towards them.

"Let's go." He leaped to his feet. If he stayed here any longer he'd die of fright.

"Jack, you must not be afraid. You are in God's care."

"I'm not scared, I'm bored."

He walked down the aisle as quickly as the dark would allow. Fear sharpened as he neared the door. He felt certain that the door would open as he approached it.

But it did not. He breathed an enormous sigh of relief as they left the church behind them.

The clock began to strike as they started down the path. Twelve o'clock. Susannah skipped in front, playing the torch on the gravestones and humming as she went. She stopped at the sound of voices.

"Did you see that, Isaac?"

"See what?"

Susannah flicked off the torch. She ran to the nearest gravestone and crouched behind it. Jack followed. She clutched at him as he knelt beside her.

Someone belched loudly. A voice boomed in to the darkness. "There was a light in the churchyard, coming towards us. I tell you

Isaac, it was plain as day. Just as the clock struck."

Susannah's face was white in the moonlight, her eyes dark and wide with fear.

"Don't worry, they won't come in," Jack whispered. "They sound too scared."

"You're too full of ale that's your trouble, Sam Daly."

"Dead man's candle, Isaac. Dead man's candle, that's what it was. You mark my words. There'll be a death to follow."

The men staggered off, bickering as they went. Susannah breathed a sigh of relief.

"Let's go," said Jack.

They came to the bottom of the lane leading to the workshop.

"Jack, you must go by yourself."

"Me?"

"Yes. Father is on watch up the lane, so I must not go."

"Oh, heck!"

"Only you can do this, Jack."

She was right. He had to get home and there was no way they'd be able to work the acorn loose without a proper tool. He took the keys and headed up the lane.

A cloud passed across the moon so that he could hardly see. He clenched the keys firmly in his fist to stop them rattling. He stumbled over something, lurched forward on to his knees and dropped the keys. They fell to the ground with a loud clatter that made him suck in his breath.

"Who goes there?"

The moon shone on Mr Roe's face so that his eyes glittered for a second. There was another man beside him. Then the lane passed into darkness again. Jack inched forward until he could close his fingers round the heavy keys. He picked them up carefully and tiptoed forward, hardly daring to breathe.

At last he reached the workshop; too far away, he hoped, for anyone to hear the grating of the key in the lock, the bumping of the door over the uneven floor. But all of these things seemed magnified a hundred times to Jack's ears, and he half expected a hand on his shoulder at any moment.

He shone his torch over the rows of tools. He had no idea what he was looking for. Eventually he picked a couple from the rack and hoped they would do the trick. Now he just had to get past the two men again.

But he needn't have worried. Mr Roe was leaning against the bill hook and seemed to be dozing. The other man sat with his back against a wall, his head on his arms. Good job the fifth cavalry's not about to invade, thought Jack.

He moved quickly, holding his breath at

every kicked pebble or heavy footstep. At last though, he saw Susannah's anxious white face peering round a cottage corner at the bottom of the lane.

"Is all well? Did you get the tools?"

"Yes, it's OK."

"I was so afraid lest I should be seen by some passer by."

"You weren't, were you?"

"No, the Lord is with us."

As Susannah pushed open her cottage door, they heard William crying.

"Oh, my. Pray that Mother has not yet heard him."

But Mother had.

Footsteps thumped on the wooden floor above, stopped, started again, moved across the floor, came downstairs.

"Susannah! Susannah!"

The girl looked at Jack in fear. Her face said, Now what?

"Where have you been, girl? What are you doing out of your bed?"

Jack saw fear twisted into the lines of Mrs Roe's face. Saw fear again as she clutched at her daughter in anger, then held on, as if for support. Her body seemed to droop.

"Forgive me, Mother." Susannah put her hand on the woman's arm. "I needed air."

The hand was shaken off impatiently and

Mrs Roe stood straight once more. She almost screamed at her daughter.

"Air indeed! Get you up the stair, my girl. I'll give you air."

Jack followed Susannah, sneaking into the bedroom quickly before Mrs Roe had a chance to shut the door on him.

"See the child, see the child! He is fevered and ill!" She almost spat the words at Susannah as if it were her fault. "God protect us all. God protect us all."

Her face crumpled and she uttered a long moan as she slumped beside the crib.

Susannah began to cry.

Chapter 11
The Nightmare Returns

The little cradle creaked on curved rockers, creak, creak, on the flagstone floor. Figures in long dresses and white bonnets surrounded it. One of them turned her face to Jack, an old face etched with lines. And down the lines ran tears. The mouth moved but there was no sound. The face pleaded with Jack but he didn't know why. Susannah ran to him, took hold of his shoulders, looked into his face.

The nightmare again: the smell of bodies; the women moving round the cradle in some strange, rhythmic dance; the stench of tallow wax; the shadows. But this was not the nightmare; this was real.

"Jack. Please help us." Susannah looked over her shoulder as she whispered the words, afraid of being caught. For who could she possibly be talking to?

Her hands dug into Jack's shoulders, their

warmth and pressure adding to the enveloping heat of the kitchen. He felt his knees fold beneath him, felt his body sink slowly to the floor in a faint. There was a rushing sound in his head. Blackness. Then the flickering of his eyelids and Susannah's face peering down into his. Her breath filled his nostrils and he moved his head sideways to escape it.

He lay on the flagstones, reassured by the cool firmness against his body. He sat up slowly. The cradle was in front of the fire, just as it had been in the dream. He could hear William's rapid breathing and see his pink face, speckled with sweat.

The movements and murmurs of the women began to make sense. He saw one of them pick up a cloth from the hearth. Each pair of eyes watched as she unwrapped it carefully. There was an onion inside, roasted by the fire. The woman picked up a spoon, and using the cloth to protect her hand from the heat, squeezed the onion hard. There was a soft, squelching sound, and then a brown liquid oozed from the squashed mess of onion, onto the spoon.

Mrs Roe lifted William from the cradle and he gave a high, irritated cry. The woman blew on the liquid to cool it, and then carefully, carefully, carried the spoon to the baby's mouth. He swallowed it without resistance or enthusiasm.

"They say 'tis a certain remedy, Hannah. May you breathe easy, knowing 'tis so."

Jack wasn't so sure about that. If it was such a certain remedy, how come so many people died? He didn't want William to be ill. He didn't want anyone to be ill or die.

"Mother, I must sleep."

Susannah's face was white, the hollows of her eyes deep and dark.

"You must indeed, child. Tomorrow you will need to watch over your brother while your father and I sleep." She spoke gently now, wearily. "To think that he should be guarding the village, tonight of all nights." She picked up a tendril of William's hair and ran it through her fingers.

"Goodnight, Mother."

"Goodnight, Susannah."

Jack perched on the end of Susannah's bed as she huddled into it, fully clothed. He was wrapped in a cloak which she had managed to smuggle upstairs for him; but it was still cold.

"I'm really stuck now, aren't I? There's nothing we can do about the cradle with all those people there."

"Is that all you can think of, boy? Yourself?" She began to cry, dragging up the sobs from deep within her body.

He was trapped in the darkness, trapped

with Susannah's sobs. And he did care. He did! It wasn't fair to say that he didn't. He had lost his best friend because of all this, he had been laughed at. He cared too much!

But that didn't mean he wanted to stay there. How could he? He didn't belong. He belonged in twentieth century Derby, and that's where he wanted to be. It was home.

"I thought you cared for William." The voice came small and accusing.

"I do! I care for him a lot! I don't want him to die, or you, or anybody. But there's nothing I can do to stop it. What can I do? What?"

He knew that he was becoming hysterical. The other, calmer Jack, the voice within him, told him to stop. But he could not. Anger poured from a boy who wanted only relief from this saturation of fear; the Jack who didn't know or understand what he was saying or why this was happening.

But then it seemed that out of the darkness of the bedroom, came a blanket of calm which wrapped itself around him. It seemed that the feelings which battled within him were being peeled away, layer by layer, until only the calm centre of him remained. Through the window, the moon and the stars appeared to spin, as though the house itself was spinning on its foundations. A voice of velvet floated round him and told him many things; told him that it was almost time; almost time. And then the voice grew fainter, the door was shut. He ran to it but there was no handle. He banged on it; but it was closed.

Now there was only a rustling in the thatch; the sound of Susannah's breathing. Jack lay on the floorboards and counted sheep. He heard the church clock strike three, strike four. He rolled over and slept.

The grass was wet with dew beneath his feet and the air sharply tinged with autumn. He looked back through the orchard, down the cottage garden and beyond it to the cottage itself. Smoke rose steadily from the chimney, the thatched roof and stone walls gleamed warmly in the sun. It was an idyllic country scene, yet Jack knew the lie that it told.

Today, Peter Halksworth was to be buried. He had never heard of him before and he was important to Jack only because he had died of the plague.

He made his way towards the pig-pen. Susannah was emptying the last of the pig's breakfast over the top of its door.

He followed her back into the house in silence. The angry shouts of the night before had given way to muted exchanges, spoken only when necessary. Strength had to be preserved he sensed, and shouting only squandered it.

"Susannah, we waited for you."

Mr and Mrs Roe sat either side of the cradle, staring into it at the sleeping William. His breathing was noisy still but he was not so restless. Or was it only the calm of morning that made it seem so?

He watched as the girl knelt to join her parents; watched and listened. He had heard only Mr Roe pray before, but now his wife and daughter gave their voices to the plea for William's life. Jack thought that if anyone had told him of this, he would have laughed; would have thought it superstitious or even ridiculous. Now he found himself adding his prayers to theirs. It was strangely comforting.

Afterwards the parents went straight to bed, leaving William in Susannah's care. They trod wearily, slowly, up the stairs. Mrs Roe stopped halfway. "If there should be the smallest change you must wake us."

They heard the bedroom door close.

"I am afraid, Jack. Afraid that he might die while I watch over him."

He didn't know what to say. The thoughts in his head didn't sound right when he tried to say them, so he said nothing.

He could attempt to go home now. There was nothing to stop him: except that any mention of his own plight seemed heartless when William lay so ill in front of him. In the end it was Susannah who made the decision; who realised, through her own sadness, that Jack had his worries too.

"I feel safer when you are here, boy. But I know that you must go. Let us do the job quickly."

He took the tools from his pocket and lay them on the floor.

"This one should do it." She took the smallest one.

"I have spent many hours watching my father at work. Sometimes he lets me help him, although mother says it is not girl's work."

Jack nodded and watched her quick fingers manipulating the tool.

"What do I care if work is man's or woman's? It is enough that I should like it." She spoke in time to the movements of her fingers. William was not disturbed by her efforts, although the cradle jarred and rocked as she worked.

"Oh!" The screwdriver slipped and a small gash appeared on the side of the acorn. "Father will have me in the stocks for this." She sat back and banged her fist on her knee.

"He won't really put you in the stocks, will he?"

"Of course not! But he will be angry that the cradle is damaged, and who could have done it but me? Not William, that is for sure."

Jack looked more closely at the gash in the wood. He followed its outline with his finger. He had noticed it before, though mellowed by age, when the cradle was at home. And he had just seen it happen. The realisation astonished him. If he ever got home he would look at that gash, and remember.

"I said it is finished, Jack. Are you listening?"

"Sorry. I was miles away."

"Look. It turns perfectly." She twirled the acorn smoothly.

"Hey, don't do that!"

"Why not?"

"You might get back to my place and I might be stuck again."

"To Derby, do you mean? In the Year of Our Lord, nineteen hundred and . . . what year was it, Jack? May I try?"

"No, you may not. What about William?"

"Poor William, I almost forgot him. He sleeps so peacefully."

He was sorry that he'd mentioned him. She'd been her usual self for the last five minutes: now she looked sad again.

"D'you mind going out, Susannah?"

"Why, boy? I should like to watch, to see what happens."

"No. No, I don't want you to."

He couldn't explain this. He just knew that he had to be by himself when he turned the

149

acorn. It was private; something that might not work if others were watching, even Susannah.

The girl walked to the door and turned, gave a little wave, face solemn. "Farewell, Jack."

"Bye."

The acorn turned: freely, smoothly, beautifully. He held his breath and waited. He felt his arms stretch wide to embrace the darkness; felt his stomach lurch at the tumbling void. "Jack, Jack, Jack," the voices whispered: but calmly, reassuringly. He could have laughed out loud.

He came to with a bump, as though someone had nudged him to one side. The cradle was rocking furiously. It was empty. Of course. But William's absence seemed larger than it had before.

He breathed in, deeply and slowly, filled with a relief so great that he had to stop himself from running through the house and shouting: I'm back! I'm back!

In any case the house was quiet. Jack crept on to the landing. The light was off and he groped his way to his own room. He reached for the clock at the side of his bed. Its luminous face told him that it was three minutes past eleven.

Could it possibly be? Could it possibly be that only two or three minutes, two or three modern, Derby minutes, had passed since he had left for Eyam? The time, in fact, that it took to walk from his own room to the crib and back? So much had happened to him in that time, yet the clock told him it had not. The clock was wrong.

Now Jack was restless. He went to the door of his parent's room and pressed his ear against it. He could hear their deep breathing.

He went downstairs to the fridge to see what he could find. Yoghurt, cheese, milk. He took the milk and went to find some cereal from the cupboard. He piled three Weetabix into a bowl and covered them with milk. He thought of another meal, eaten three hundred years ago.

As he ate, he became aware of a vague feeling of disappointment. I suppose, he thought, I was expecting police cars with flashing lights. And Mum being brave while she told a TV reporter about the last time she'd seen me, and what I was wearing. He sighed. Tiredness had crept up on him, unobserved. He pushed the bowl away and dragged himself upstairs.

No time passes while I'm in Eyam, he told himself. No one missed me because as far as they're concerned, I'm not missing. And that seems to apply whether I've been away for two minutes or two days. He threw his clothes on to the floor, dived under the duvet, and slept.

His dreams were filled with smoke-filled

kitchens and women in bonnets and babies crying. One of the women was his mother, wearing a bonnet and a long, brown dress. She picked the baby out of the crib, and the baby was Jack. Once, he was woken by his own shouts and once, towards morning, he dreamed that Susannah walked into his bedroom and told him that it was too late. The voices stole into his dreams and whispered to him; told him that now was the time. "Are you ready, Jack?" they asked. "Are you ready now?"

When he woke in the morning he was cold, stiff and tired. He was also ready: ready to carry out the task that had been his all along. He didn't know what it involved, but he did know that the first step was to find out as much as he could about the plague. Somehow, through the long hours of his broken sleep, he had been told this. For the moment at least, that was sufficient.

He had to stop himself from throwing his arms round Mum. Even Dad looked quite loveable. He felt as though he'd been away for weeks and weeks and he was so glad to see them both: though this didn't divert him from what he had to do.

"If plague happened today, could you cure it?" He looked from one to the other of his parents: they both looked puzzled.

"Plague? D'you mean bubonic plague?" Mum's forehead looked as ridged as a ploughed field.

"Give us a break, Jack. It's quarter to eight on a cold and frosty morning and you want to know all the medical intricacies of plague." Dad shook his newspaper vigorously.

"I don't want to know all the medical intricacies. I just want to know if you can cure it, that's all." Jack knew that Dad's clever-clever answer was a sure sign that he hadn't a clue about the plague but didn't want to admit it.

"Well, it's not the sort of thing you come across nowadays; it's almost unheard of. I wouldn't know where to start. But there's a history of medicine textbook in the surgery. I'll find it for you."

Mum left the book on his bed after breakfast and he made himself late for school reading it. He'd not understood all of it, but that didn't matter. He understood the most important thing of all; plague was curable now, with antibiotics.

He cast his mind back to his days in infant school when he'd been learning to read. One of his favourite games had been to sit on Mum's knee while she sorted the stuff out of the surgery cupboards. He'd looked at the bottles and packets with their impossible names, had listened to Mum pronouncing them for him, had tried to copy her. He couldn't remember now, when he'd reached the stage where he could reel off those impossible names by heart, read and pronounce them as well as any doctor or pharmacist. But those names were as familiar to him as the nursery rhymes he'd learned earlier. And one of them held the key to the plague.

He had spent the day at school imagining William, sick and fretful, surrounded by keening women. He imagined too, the medicine in his parents' surgery. He saw the two images merge as they had been meant to do all along. He understood this now.

So he had come home from school knowing what he had to do, yet not knowing whether he should do it. Now he sat with his parents in the sitting room, sorting through some old photographs. They were laughing and remembering.

"Is it always wrong to steal?" The question dropped awkwardly into his parents' laughter, its seriousness out of kilter with their mood.

"Oh, Jack," his father groaned, and rolled on to the carpet. "The meaning of life, death and the universe."

Mum laughed even more.

"I'm serious." Things were coming to a

pretty pass when you couldn't rely on your parents to behave like responsible human beings. He tried again. "Is it always wrong to steal?"

"We . . . ell." Dad sat up and clasped his arms round his knees. "It's almost always wrong to steal, but in some circumstances you might have no choice."

"What sort of circumstances?" Jack sat to attention.

"Well, if you're starving for instance." Mum leaned against Dad's knees and he pretended to collapse with the weight. They started giggling again.

Honestly! If this was the way I behaved when they were trying to talk to me, it'd be nag, nag, nag. Jack knew that at any other time he'd have joined in; but this was something that had to be sorted out, and quickly. "This is serious! Be serious can't you?"

"Sorry, Jack, sorry." Mum struggled to her knees and lifted her hands in a "don't shoot" gesture.

"So if you're starving, it's right to steal food?"

"No, not right exactly, but not wrong either. It certainly wasn't right that starving children, no older than you, used to be hanged for stealing food."

"Mum, you're joking! You mean they were

really hanged?"

"I'm not joking and yes, they were really hanged."

"Well, if a thing's not wrong, then it must be right, mustn't it?" Jack was puzzled.

"Sometimes it is, sometimes it's difficult to know. As Dad says, it depends on the circumstances."

"If I were dying," he was gratified to see both of his parents listening intently, "And the only way you could get the medicine to cure me was by stealing it, would you steal it?"

"Yes." They spoke together. The answer was definite, immediate: and what's more they'd virtually given him the go-ahead.

He would carry out the next part of his task after they'd gone to bed.

Chapter 12
A Small Burglary

Jack lay fully dressed on top of his bed. What he had to do was quite simple. He went through it step by step: he would go downstairs to the surgery, find the medicine, come back upstairs to the baby's room, turn the knob on the cradle, arrive in Eyam and give the medicine to William. Easy peasy; no problem.

Then why did his legs go all wobbly every time he tried to stand up? Why was his stomach doing Olympic somersaults?

Because I'm a coward, he told himself; that's why. They're my friends and they need help. Besides, if I don't do something, William will die; and if I do, he might just live.

But no matter how hard he tried to reason with himself, his mind still came back to the same old problem: over and over. He was about to steal, to become a thief. What was worse, he was about to steal from his own father.

"But William is dying!" His own shout startled him.

"Dying, dying, dying," the voices sighed.

"Stop it! Go away! Get someone else to do it!" He pushed his fists against his ears to try and block out the whispers, but they were inside his head and would not go away. "Jack, Jack, Jack. Quickly, Jack. Go quickly." The ceiling of his bedroom became a black sky peppered with ice-white stars. The door was opening; opening wide. The door had a handle. The choice was his.

He didn't remember getting to his feet or leaving his room. He didn't remember making the decision either. But the decision had been made. He had to try to save William.

He padded across the landing to his parents' room and listened. Mum was giving funny little groans: probably dreaming. All quiet now. The coast was clear.

Down the stairs, past the first door, on to the second. Turn the key slowly, slowly. Push open the door; hardly a sound. Walk to the cupboard, turn the key, open the door. Open the door, Jack, open the door. But it would not open. He pushed and turned, pushed and turned, till his fingers were sore.

"Come on! Open will you; open!" He could feel his breath start to catch in his throat and wheeze its way out. His heart banged in his chest. "Come on!"

Click. The key turned. He had been turning it the wrong way. Stupid! He opened the cupboard carefully, hardly daring to breathe. There was a number of packets and bottles inside. He examined their labels: not this one, not this, not this, not this. Don't say there isn't any. Please don't say there isn't any. He picked up a pile of small boxes, bound together with an elastic band. Yes! This was it!

His hands were shaking as he put the boxes on the desk and pulled the elastic band from around them. He counted them, five sachets in each box, and each sachet with just the right dose. He'd done his homework carefully. He'd need four boxes.

The sound came just as he was turning to leave. At first he thought he'd imagined it. He held his breath. There it was again. A muffled bumping from the room above. And now footsteps; footsteps crossing the bedroom floor, a door opening, footsteps crossing the landing, another door opening.

Jack stood rigid with fear. His hands were sweaty with panic. The footsteps were coming downstairs.

"Jack! Where are you?"

Hide the boxes. Quick! Hide the boxes.

He pushed the medicine into the waste bin,

just as the door opened. His face was flushed
with guilt as he looked from his father to the
bin, then back again. Don't look at the bin,
idiot. You'll give the game away. He could
have kicked himself. He'd never make a
burglar.

"What the heck are you doing in here? Why
aren't you in your pyjamas?"

What could he say?

"I came to get the history of medicine book. I
wanted to look at it again." Brilliant, Jack,
brilliant. He had to stop himself from grinning.

"Well, get into bed, and be quick about it.
You know you're not supposed to be in here.
And listen. The baby's on its way. A bit early,
but never mind that."

Oh no! Of all the times in the world to
choose, she has to choose now. He felt like
running upstairs and telling her to hang on.
But somewhere at the back of his mind, he was
aware that babies are born when they're good
and ready; not a minute sooner or later.

"I'm just going to phone Alison to come and
stay with you. We'll need to get to the hospital
fairly soon. Lock the door after you."

Jack waited until Dad had gone, and then
retrieved the medicine from its hiding place.
He pushed the boxes up his jumper, and
hoped that Dad was back in his own room.

He thumped upstairs miserably. He'd

known that Alison would be coming to stay but that didn't make it any easier. Why did it have to happen tonight? Why?

He trudged to his own room and hid the boxes under his duvet. They'd be safe there until he needed them. But first he had to see Mum.

"Mum, can I come in?" He poked his head round the bedroom door and saw that she was pulling on her coat. "Are you all right?"

"Yes, course I am. Someone, somewhere, is having a baby every second of every day."

And every second of every day, someone is dying, thought Jack, and saw the cradle, rocking and empty.

Mum smiled at him. "Cheer up. It's not fatal, you know."

But he heard her suck in her breath sharply, saw the smile disappear from her face.

"Beddy-byes, Jack. See you in the morning." She unscrewed her face and smiled; he knew it was a smile just for him, to make him feel better.

"Bye, Mum. Good luck."

"Bye, Sugar."

Sugar! She called him that only in her very soppiest moods. He smiled to himself as he felt the tears prick at his eyes. She'd be all right.

"Will she be all right, Dad?"

"Course she will, son. In a few hours it will

all be over and you'll have your sibling." He
ruffled Jack's hair.

"Sibling?"

"Brother or sister to you, mate." He winked
and they smiled at each other. Sibling! Made it
sound like a frog.

So, he thought, Mum's going to hospital and
I'm going to Eyam. She's going to have a baby
and I'm going to save one, I hope. Funny that.

Alison arrived in a flurry of importance and
an air of 'don't worry, I've got everything
under control'. She went straight to the spare
room, after despatching Jack to bed with
exclamations of horror at his pyjamaless state.
Now she'd be bedding down for the night, he
thought. Or perhaps just getting her
broomstick and black cat organised.

Jack was relieved she was out of the way. He
certainly didn't want to spend a minute longer
than he had to with Alison. And he wanted to
go to Eyam.

The cradle waited for him. It seemed to Jack, as
he knelt beside it, that the darkness was filled
with his fears. And his fears were interwoven
and confused; they had merged into one large
and unpleasant feeling that he couldn't attach
to anything in particular, though everything
was tainted with it.

His fear of going back to Eyam had lain

unfocussed in his mind. But now the memory returned; the memory of being trapped, out of his own place and time. And he had to face that fear. He had to go back, scared or not.

If William died, at least he would know he'd done his best to save him. Stealing the medicine was wrong: in Jack's mind there was no getting round that: but he'd done it for the right reason. And he'd made the right decision. He tightened his fingers on the four boxes, bound safely with the elastic band once more.

A curious feeling of well-being settled upon him. It was time now; time to carry out his task. He turned the acorn.

The tunnel of rushing wind sucked him into itself. He was absorbed by the blackness and the voices were very close. Hands reached out to him. Someone stroked his face. Then Susannah's voice.

"Jack! You startled me."

The kitchen was just as he'd left it. William breathed noisily in his cradle and Susannah was alone with him.

"Where's your Mother and Father?"

"Sleeping still. I am glad you came so soon."

"Soon?"

"Time for the church clock to have struck nine and ten: no more."

Only an hour or so then: there was no accounting for it.

"I brought these." He held out the boxes and fished in his pocket for the plastic measuring spoon he'd taken from the kitchen drawer.

"It's medicine for William. You must give him one of these sachets twice a day; one in the morning and one in the evening. You can use this spoon. And you must use all the sachets, even if he seems better."

"What is it?" She took the boxes and twanged at the elastic band with her finger, a smile spreading across her face as she did so. "See, Jack, how it becomes long then short again. May I keep it?"

"It's just an old elastic band. Why don't you listen to what I'm telling you?" Why did she always concentrate on the wrong things? "D'you want William to get better or not?"

"Of course I do, boy." She put the elastic band into the pocket of her apron; carefully, as if it were something special. She picked up one of the boxes again. "But what is it?" She frowned at the writing on the packet, then held it at arm's length and looked at it suspiciously.

"It's medicine and it ought to make William better. Don't you trust me?" The girl might at least show some gratitude after all the trouble he'd taken to get it.

"Will it really make him well again?" She looked eager and there was hope in her face.

"Well," he thought quickly; he wasn't going

to make promises that he might not be able to keep. "It should do."

"Jack, you are an angel."

"Yeah, that's what my Mum says," said Jack, embarrassed.

"I mean a real angel, sent from God."

Oh heck, there she goes again. He could feel himself blushing and bent over William to hide his face.

"Better start the medicine straight away. You sit William on your knee and I'll give it to him." He straightened up and began bustling about to try to cover the fact that he wanted to cry. Honestly, Jack Rutherford, he scolded himself, you've cried more in the last few weeks than in the whole of your life. You're turning into a grisly little wimp.

"He's very hot." Jack could feel the heat from the baby's body without touching him.

He wondered later, how it was that he'd known what to do. He'd seemed to know instinctively that William must be cooled down, that his temperature was dangerous.

He fetched the bucket from the side of the hearth. For once he had a clean handkerchief and he dipped it into the water. It was surprisingly cold, given the heat of the kitchen.

Susannah lifted William from the cradle and wiped his face with the corner of her apron. But when she saw that Jack was about to use cold water, she snatched William away from him.

"What are you doing, boy? He will take a chill and then he will die for sure."

"Listen, Susannah. It's important to get his temperature down."

"His what?"

"His body heat. He's too hot and that's dangerous. We can cool him down with cold water."

"No! I will not be responsible for William's death."

"Just trust me. Just try." He searched frantically for the right words. What could he say? "You said I was an angel from God. Well, I am. Do as you're told."

"Then I am right." Her face relaxed and Jack felt ashamed. But it was the only way. It was William's life that mattered now.

The girl watched as Jack sat on the bench beside her and wiped the little boy's face. He moved slightly, but hardly protested.

"You must do this regularly, to keep his temp . . . his body heat down." Jack didn't know how he knew this, but he felt certain it was the right thing to do. Perhaps he'd heard his parents discussing it. "Promise me, Susannah."

"As you say."

But she might not. She might forget, or not

realise how important it is. Jack thought hard. How could he make sure she carried on with the treatment?

"Susannah?"

"Yes, Jack?"

"I want you to give me your solemn oath that you will carry on with the cooling treatment. But above all," he could hear his father's voice now, echoed in his own, "Give William all the medicine, until all the little sachets are used up. Even if you think he's better. Swear on the bible."

"I will do no such thing, boy! It is a shameful sin to swear on the bible."

Got it wrong again, Jack. He sighed.

"Well, give me your solemn oath, then."

"I give you my solemn oath, that I will give William all the medicine and bathe him in cold water." She shuddered. "And I will pray that the cold water shall not harm him."

Jack's hand shook as he took the first sachet from its box. He'd not thought to bring scissors. Hope it tears all right, he thought. He put the corner of the sachet into his mouth and pulled at it with his teeth. The wrapping tore easily and he tasted the medicine on the tip of his tongue.

"Bananas," he said.

"What?" The girl frowned.

"Bananas. That's what it tastes of."

167

"Bananas?" The frown deepened.

"Oh, never mind. D'you think you'll be able to open them by yourself?"

Susannah nodded.

Jack emptied the medicine on to the spoon and carried it carefully to William's mouth. He mustn't spill any. There was no more where this came from.

The little boy sucked at the liquid appreciatively, the first real response he'd shown for quite a while.

Susannah smiled at Jack. "He likes it."

"It's specially for children and it tastes nice."

"Of bananas, whatever that is. And this will make him well, you say?"

"I'm not promising, but there's a good chance."

Jack rubbed his face on his sleeve. It was stifling in here, he didn't know how they could stand it. Susannah didn't seem a bit bothered by it though.

He wiped his face again; he was sticky with sweat. He'd got a bit of a headache as well. Must be all the worry. But he'd done what he came to do and there was no point in staying.

"I'm going home now."

"But you have only just arrived."

He needed to find out about Mum, although he knew that however long he stayed in Eyam, it would make no difference to what time he got home; only a minute or so would have passed. But the time goes slowly when I'm here and I want it to go quickly so I can see Mum again.

"I have to go. My Mum's having a baby any time."

"That is good, Jack." Susannah smiled with pleasure. "Has she a good woman to attend her?"

Well, there was the midwife he supposed; or the madwife, as Mum always called her. And the doctors. Were they men or women? Did it matter?

"Yeah, I expect there'll be plenty of women."

Susannah nodded her head. "That is good, boy; very good. May God deliver her safely and give the child long life."

Sometimes you sound like a wise old woman, Susannah Roe. But Amen, anyway.

"Jack?" She was frowning, her forehead raised into ridges.

"What?"

"Angels do not have parents. There is no marriage in heaven."

Oh heck! He thought quickly. "Well, I'm not a real angel. But I was sent here to help you." And it was true. The only reason for any of this was to help William.

She looked as though she was about to argue, but William began to whimper. She leaned over to him and spoke soothingly. The little boy settled and she turned to Jack once more.

"Thank you, Jack. Thank you for your help."

Susannah knelt by the crib and rocked it gently, so that it creaked on the flagstones. Her face was upturned to Jack's. Her eyes seemed bluer than usual and her skin pink against the white of her bonnet.

"You'd better clear off now."

"Clear off?" The girl frowned.

"Go, depart, scram, scarper." He grinned as she scurried for the door.

"Farewell, Jack. And God bless you."

"That's OK." He stood up quickly; too quickly. His head swarmed with dizziness. He put his hand on the table to steady himself until it cleared.

"Are you all right, Jack?"

"Yes, go away."

The last he saw of her was her face looking into his, as if she didn't want to let him go. She was in shadow; her eyes less blue, her skin darker.

"Bye, Susannah." He looked once more at the sleeping infant, his body framed by the wooden cradle. He looked peaceful. "Bye, little William."

He turned the acorn and felt himself falling. He closed his eyes and saw the kitchen again.

He saw Susannah kneeling by the cradle and gazing into it at William, sleeping. The firelight fell on their faces and made them glow. The darkness moved in on them, eating up the details of the kitchen until only their faces were left, framed in a circle of light.

Chapter 13
A Very Unusual Illness

"It's a boy!"

It was Dad's voice; and Dad's hand on his shoulder, shaking him gently.

"It's a boy, Jack. You've got a baby brother."

Through the sluggishness of sleep, Jack picked up the chuckle in Dad's voice and chuckled with him; a deep-in-the-duvet, half-asleep chuckle. He struggled up the bed and peered into the half-light of morning. Dad reached out to him and ruffled his hair.

A boy; a brother; a pain in the elbow. Jack collapsed on to Dad and the two of them laughed together as if they'd just heard the world's funniest joke. A brother. Jack rolled over. A brother. He smiled into his pillow-case.

The house seemed asleep. The kitchen was empty. Alison was still in bed and Dad was getting ready for work. He would have a week's holiday when Mum came out of hospital. Jack hoped it was soon and then Alison could go home. Fat lot of use she was, anyway. Where was his breakfast for a start? He plugged in the kettle and rummaged among the cereal packets for something appealing. Nothing was. It was cold outside and he fancied porridge, but he couldn't be bothered to make it.

Truth was, his headache was starting up again and he was beginning to feel hot and cold both at the same time. If he had a cold he'd be able to stay off school. If he timed it right, they could all be at home together. He wished Mum was at home now; he didn't feel too good. His head throbbed and his throat hurt. His skin prickled as if someone was tapping him with sharp thorns.

Dad came humming into the kitchen and clattered around in the dresser. Jack held on to the edge of the cooker and winced at the noise of a cereal bowl banging onto the table.

"Not eaten yet?"

Jack heard the rustling of cornflakes, and the swish of milk poured over them. A spoon clanged.

"No, not yet." Breakfast didn't seem like a good idea any more.

He turned from the cooker and calculated the distance to the nearest chair. He had to concentrate hard to reach it. He had to think about what his feet were doing and make sure that his body stayed upright while they were doing it. It wasn't easy. He pulled out the chair which seemed heavier than usual, and half fell into it.

"Careful, Jack, you're like a baby elephant. Talking of babies, I've no idea what we're going to call this little brother of yours. Any suggestions?" Dad rattled on and on. It was only when Jack slipped sideways from his chair that he noticed anything wrong with him.

"Are you all right?"

Dad's voice came from somewhere above Jack's head. It echoed another voice, asking the same question, a long, long time ago. Had it been in this kitchen? Or the other one? Which was which? He didn't know. The two kitchens had merged and become one, filled with the people from both worlds. Mrs Roe and Mum, side by side, peering into a cauldron.

"Jack, what's the matter?"

He was aware of Dad's breath on his face. He was aware of the clock, ticking time away. Somehow, the seat of his chair was above his head and he was holding onto the leg. Why was he lying down? Why was Dad looking at him like that?

He made the journey through the hall with Dad's arm under his, holding him up. The stairs came up to meet him and Dad pulled him away from them until he was almost upright, dragging his feet up and up the stairs. Familiar objects seemed to sail past him: pictures on the wall, the pattern of the carpet, his bedroom door, kicked open by Dad's foot: bang! Everything was too loud, too loud. Everything was too hot. And then pillows, cool at first, but hot too quickly. Something pushed into his mouth, cold and glassy.

Time was no longer measured. There was no getting up or going to bed, no school; no meals even. There were no little parcels of routine to mark time's passing. There was pain and heat and a feeling of illness that made him aware of hardly anything else. He concentrated on being ill; it absorbed him totally so that there was nothing beyond it. Nothing except images, impressions.

Faces appeared and disappeared as he watched them. The faces of all those he cared about danced through his mind, smiling and waving, like actors taking their final curtain call. There were Susannah and William; there was Tom as he used to be, grinning and friendly; there were Mr and Mrs Roe, forever busy, forever serious; there was Mum, holding the baby with its unseen face. And there was Dad.

He tried to tell Dad about Eyam and the crib. It was vital that he should understand because he would have to take over now; there was nothing more that Jack could do. Sometimes he spoke his urgent messages to Susannah as she stood next to Dad at the bedside. How had she come here? Where was William? Why wouldn't Dad speak to her? But then she would fade away and Dad would smile and stroke Jack's hair and nod. He was so calm, so understanding, so reassuring.

Jack became used to Dad's comforting presence. But sometimes he would wake to find him gone. And then the fear would come; the fear that he might die; the fear that William had already done so. Jack knew that he was having the same medicine as William; there was the same sweet smell of bananas, the same pale yellow stickiness. He had not died yet. Perhaps William, more than three hundred years ago, had not died yet.

And then Susannah stood beside him again, holding William in her arms and laughing. Sometimes he was back in the nightmare kitchen with the flickering shadows. Sometimes he didn't know where he was.

Then one morning Jack woke and knew the illness had abated. He felt as though he had been ill for a long, long time and yet he had no sense of how long. Weeks perhaps?

"Two days," said Dad, sitting on the bed.

"Two days? I thought it would take longer

than that."

"Why?"

"Oh, nothing." He waited for Dad to say something, to tell him that he'd had a very unusual illness; one not much heard of nowadays. But Dad just stood up and yawned.

Jack looked at him and saw, in a rush of sympathy, that he looked tired, looked suddenly older. It occurred to him that his illness must have been a strain for Dad. What with that and having to visit Mum and the baby, he couldn't have had much sleep lately.

"I told you about Eyam and everything, didn't I?"

"Yes, you did. Very interesting it was too."

"Is that all?"

Dad looked puzzled. "Well, it has to be said you've got a powerful imagination. You take after your mother, there."

Jack could hardly believe what he was hearing. What was Dad talking about? Why couldn't he just come out and say what had really been the matter with him?

"You certainly don't take after me," Dad went on, "Not an ounce of imagination in my body. Good thing too. Somebody has to have their feet on the ground in this family."

So that was to be the little game, was it? They were to pretend, apparently, that Jack had been ill with a perfectly ordinary, modern germ, leading to a perfectly ordinary, modern temperature. And temperatures sometimes cause hallucinations. If the truth lay somewhere else, no one was going to admit it; especially not Dad. There was to be a conspiracy of silence. Jack folded his arms angrily across his chest.

"By the way, I bumped into Mr Nixon in town." Dad seemed not to have noticed Jack's anger. Either that or he was ignoring it. "He told me about your essay. He was very impressed."

Jack studied the pattern on his duvet cover.

"I told him you appeared to be somewhat gripped by the subject."

Oh yes, Father dear, I am somewhat gripped by the subject. Ever so somewhat gripped! He wished he could say it out loud, but Dad had been great just lately. And Jack didn't want to spoil things, despite his frustration.

"You kept rambling on about it. Fevers can play amazing tricks on the mind. Cup of tea?"

Dad closed the bedroom door behind him and Jack was left to ponder the mysteries of adult behaviour.

So. Dismissed as a trick of the mind. All that had happened to him, a trick of the mind. Jack sighed. Why wouldn't Dad believe him? Why wouldn't he believe the truth? Perhaps people believed what suited them and ignored the rest. Anyway, Dad was wrong about the temperature. He'd started going to Eyam ages ago, when his temperature had been absolutely normal. Dad would just have to believe what he wanted, there was nothing Jack could do about it. Adults just thought they knew it all.

There was a knock. "Room service." Tom's head poked round the bedroom door. "Tea up."

"Tom!"

"Hi." He was struggling with a pile of books, a brown paper bag and a mug of tea. "Your Dad said to go and get some books for you. And this is from me."

"Thanks." Jack took the bag and opened it. Grapes. "Thanks, Tom." He patted the bed for Tom to sit down.

"I'll stand up if you don't mind."

Jack sipped at his tea. It was hot and made his throat feel sore again.

There was an awkward silence.

Tom wandered round the bedroom, picking things up and putting them down again. "So . . . how are you?"

"Fine, fine. Well . . . nearly. You know."

Tom was picking through a pile of cassettes. He turned round to face Jack. "I'm sorry." He said it too quickly, as if to have done with it.

"It's OK." And it was. Tom was part of the

179

ordinary, everyday world. A world which seemed safe and which Jack wanted to be part of again. And he needed Tom's friendship.

"I got really scared, you know. You really spooked me." He picked at a loose thread on his jumper. "Sorry."

"It's OK." Did that mean Tom didn't believe him? Did he think it was some sort of creepy game he'd been playing? Maybe he did believe him and that's why he'd been scared. Who knew? Tom's thoughts would have to remain in Tom's head. Jack wasn't going to risk asking about them.

"You know something?" Tom sat on the very edge of the bed.

"What?"

"Simon Smith's boring." He glanced at Jack and grinned.

"I could have told you that." Jack grinned back.

"He's not like us," said Tom. "Me and you think the same."

"I thought we found that out years ago."

"Yeah, we did, didn't we?"

"You were always a bit of a thicko."

"Watch it, Rutherford, or I'll beat you up."

"But I'm an invalid," croaked Jack.

They laughed then and it made things easier. After a while they were chatting as though nothing had ever happened.

Some time later Dad's head poked round the door. "Mustn't exhaust the patient, you know."

Tom got up to go.

"Oh, Dad. I'm all right, now."

But after Tom had gone, Jack realised that Dad was right. Even getting up to go to the loo seemed too much of an effort.

As he drifted into sleep he thought about how much better he felt about things now that he and Tom were friends again. Even if he couldn't talk about Eyam.

He didn't feel better for long, though. He was dozing when the door opened and Dad walked in. He swept his arms open in a grand gesture.

"Surprise, surprise!"

"Mum!"

It was a thinner Mum who stood in the doorway, the bump transferred to her arms. "Sorry you've been ill, Number One Son. Would you like to see Number Two?" She turned the much wrapped bundle towards him so that he saw a scrunched-up blob of pink flesh which he presumed to be the face of his brother.

"It's ugly."

"Come on, Jack," Dad barked irritably as he left the room.

Come on, Jack. He echoed Dad's words to

himself. Come on what? It's the truth. That is one ugly baby. He wriggled further down the bed so that he didn't have to look at it. Or Mum.

"Sorry, Jack," said Mum, placatingly. "I daren't come any nearer with the baby. We don't know what's been wrong with you and I should hate him to catch anything."

"It's all right for me to catch things, then," said Jack, unreasonably. "I don't suppose you care very much about that."

And you might not know what's been wrong with me, he thought. But I do.

To Jack's annoyance he felt his voice catch, and tears pricking too easily at his eyes. He rubbed at them and hoped Mum hadn't noticed. He didn't want her to think he was bothered by a puny ratscrap of a baby.

"I care very much, Jack."

He noticed, with surprise, that Mum's voice sounded slightly wobbly, too. He pressed his advantage. "Why did you bring it? Why couldn't you just come and see me by yourself?"

"I'm sorry, Jack. I should have done."

"Yes, you should." He pressed his face into the pillow like a two year old.

It was quiet. He could hear the sound of traffic on the road outside and the tick of his alarm clock on the bedside table. He risked a glance. She was leaning against the door, crying. Crying quietly into the baby's bonnet, just as Susannah had cried into William's.

"I'm sorry, Mum."

"I'm sorry, too, Jack; sorry you've been so ill. And I should have known better." She looked down at the baby. "It was thoughtless of me when you're feeling so rough."

She disappeared and Jack could hear her footsteps along the landing. He heard them come back again and into the bedroom. He felt the sag of the bed as she sat down beside him, minus the baby.

And then they were both crying and saying they were sorry. They helped each other to tissues and smiled at each other through their tears.

Then they were quiet together. They sat for a long time saying nothing. Jack tried not to think about the baby, but its presence seemed to dominate the house.

"What are you going to call it?" He couldn't bring himself to say he.

Mum smiled. "We can't decide. He's just it and he at the moment."

"Oh." Perhaps if it didn't have a name, it wouldn't really exist. He didn't want it to have a name.

It was quiet again. Then, "Mum?"

"Yes?"

Jack paused. "Oh, nothing." There was no point. He couldn't tell her about Eyam. There was no one who would listen to his worries about William. No one he could tell, after all. But there never had been really. There was nothing new in that.

"Well, I can't stay here all day, much as I'd like to." Mum stood up. "You know, Jack, I'm so pleased you persuaded me to buy that crib. The baby looks just right in it."

Huh, thought Jack.

She went out of the room and came straight back in again. "I forgot to tell you, talking of cradles. You know that loose acorn?"

Jack nodded. His heart began to thump ominously against his ribs.

"You haven't seen it, have you? Dad's hunted high and low for it. It looks as though we've lost it," said Mum, stating the obvious. "And you know what that means."

Jack looked out of the window, at nothing. His mind was racing. He knew all too well what losing the acorn meant.

"It means the crib will be spoiled. It'll look odd. Well, I don't know where it's got to. It seems to have disappeared completely."

Jack said nothing. What was there to say? He would never see Susannah or William again. It was the end of everything.

Chapter 14
Saying Goodbye to Susannah

They never did find the acorn. As Jack recovered, he spent hours looking for it. But it had, as Mum said, completely disappeared. Jack tried to draw comfort from the fact. If the acorn had parted company with the cradle, then no one else could ever do what he had done. The plague would stay in history's memory. It would not return to haunt the present. And surely its disappearance must mean that he'd been successful; that William was better?

But Jack's attempts to reason things through did not prevent him from standing by the cradle whenever the baby was out of it, willing it to take him back to Eyam again. The cradle refused. He tried to turn the other three acorns, but they remained stubbornly fixed.

Then Jack decided that if he could not go back to the seventeenth century, he would have to content himself with the twentieth. Eyam still existed so he could go there. Who knows what he might find? As far as Jack was concerned the story was unfinished. And he had to know the end.

The opportunity came towards the end of term, when Jack had been back at school for a week or so. Mr Nixon had set them an essay for homework and Dad had pounced on Jack's English book, wanting to read the famous story. Mum had read it too.

But Jack had been annoyed. It felt like an invasion of his privacy. He wouldn't have minded if they'd been prepared to believe it was not made up; but it was just a story to them; an imaginative story that led them to fantasize about Jack's future career as a writer.

"You talked about Eyam all the time you were ill, apparently." Mum was feeding the baby and Jack was looking at some old Beanos he'd found in the shed. He'd not read them for years but now they seemed secure and comforting, although he couldn't think why.

"Yeah, Dad told me. High temperature, he said."

"I'll give Mr Nixon his due," Mum went on, "He certainly knows how to make a subject interesting. Your enthusiasm just leaps off the page." She nodded towards the English book. "It's almost as if you were really in Eyam." She looked at Jack quizzically. "We must go there, as you're so interested in the place. I'd like to see it again myself, and there won't be much chance once I'm back at work."

"Could we? When? On Saturday?"

"OK. Saturday it is."

"Promise?"

"Promise."

It would be their day. Just his and Mum's.

Jack's hand was on the car door when he noticed the baby in its carrycot on the back seat. He hadn't seen very much of it one way or another. Mum and Dad had been worried at first that he might still be infectious. Then he went back to school and when he came home Mum would be busy feeding or changing it. She seemed to be the baby's mother now; not his.

He glared at his mother over the car roof. "Why couldn't Dad look after it? I thought this was going to be our trip."

The two doors slammed in unison and the car pulled out of the drive and on to the main road.

Jack had assumed that there would be just the two of them; like it used to be. Anger bubbled in his chest.

"I couldn't possibly leave the baby for a whole day. He has to be fed every three or four hours, you know that. And I'm the only one can do it."

There was no reply.

"He's just had a feed, so we should have some time to ourselves before he starts squawking again."

Still no reply.

"When he's older, when I'm not feeding him any more, we'll go out by ourselves; just the two of us." Mum patted his knee and smiled at him.

Jack lifted a corner of his mouth, but it could hardly be called a smile.

As mile followed mile, Jack's anger subsided. He found himself thinking back over the last couple of weeks. Dad still believed his story was due to a high temperature and a love of history. He wasn't so sure about Mum. She had asked him which book it was that had told the story of the Roe family. Could she get it from the library? He had mumbled something about not being able to remember. But part of him wanted her to know, to understand what it had been like, to see Susannah and William through his eyes. And sometimes he thought she did know. Or was he imagining it? His experience was an isolating one because now there was a large part of him that he couldn't share with anyone. And that felt lonely.

"I hope you won't be disappointed, Jack."

Disappointed? That hadn't occurred to him. But the thought was worrying. What if he arrived to find Eyam a completely different village? Not his Eyam at all?

"It's just that sometimes things are better in the imagination than they are in reality."

Imagination. Jack chewed on his thumbnail. No, imagination had nothing to do with it and he was not going to let Mum, or anyone else, try to convince him that it had. But it all seemed such a long time ago. He had to work hard to hang on to the certainty that it had been real; was real still.

He looked out of the window at the familiar countryside. He was apprehensive, in the same way as before a test at school; the same sort of light, fluttering feeling in his stomach.

"Not far now." Mum's voice interrupted the silence.

The car rounded a bend and Chatsworth House, elegant and remote, drew Jack's eye forcibly into itself. He could not look away from it. It demanded his eyes.

The car slowed to a crawl as a wandering sheep ambled across the road in front of them.

Jack looked at his mother and thought of the things he knew that she didn't. It seemed to him that he understood much more than his parents. But by the time he grew to their age he might not understand anything of what he

THE NAMING OF WILLIAM RUTHERFORD

knew now. It was hard to believe that adults had ever been kids; that kids really grew into adults. At times they seemed like members of a different species, not younger and older versions of the same one.

It's all to do with time, he thought. Adults think they know more because they've lived longer. They think they know what it's like for kids, but they don't really. Childhood must seem to them like a place they once lived in, ages ago. He looked at Mum, lost in concentration. What was it like to be her? Jack knew that she always tried to understand him. But he also knew that children understood things which adults had forgotten.

"I think kids know more than adults sometimes. They understand more, in a funny sort of way," he murmured.

"What?" Mum wrinkled her eyebrows. She'd been concentrating on the narrow, bendy lanes and keeping the car out of ditches. "What brought this on?"

"Oh, nothing. Just thinking about time."

"We're not late, are we?"

"No, Mum." Jack sighed. "Not that sort of time."

"You mean time as in past, present and future?"

"Yes."

Time. The past. Most people, thought Jack,

assume that people in the past didn't know very much. But that's not true. They knew a lot of things the people of today don't know any more. He thought of Susannah and her family and how wise they all seemed, even though they didn't have a proper loo or a telly or car. They seemed to know something he didn't, some sort of secret that he couldn't quite grasp.

"You're really into this history thing, aren't you?"

Jack grunted.

"I'm glad. I used to love history when I was at school. Still do, come to think of it."

"And you're in a time warp," said Jack. "Nobody says, 'really into,' any more. Only wrinklies."

Mum gave him a sideways swipe and Jack grinned.

"Seriously though," she said, "history and time are fascinating, aren't they? I think I understand what a hundred years means. But I don't really. I understand what a hundred means, as a number, but I can't ever know what a hundred years feels like."

"I thought you were a hundred, Mum."

Another sideways swipe, and then, "Well, you're in a time warp too, Jack. In forty years time, nobody will say wrinkly any more. Only wrinklies like yourself, as you will be by then."

"Time's funny, isn't it?"

Mum nodded. "It certainly is."

"I used to think that time went forward in a straight line: yesterday, today, tomorrow and the day after. Like a march that goes on for ever."

"The march of time." Mum smiled.

"But some of the marchers stop and turn back. The places they passed through are still there; they go back and visit them. D'you understand? D'you see?"

"Yes, yes, I do see. But it's more a question of place than time, isn't it?"

Time and place, place and time. How were they linked? How did they fit together?

"We're here."

Mum indicated right, and Jack saw the signpost as they turned. Only half a mile! He felt the tension mount as they drove up and round, up and round. They followed the sign for the carpark, and stopped there.

Jack looked. It seemed familiar, yet he couldn't say why. There was nothing he recognised.

"It's years since I've been here."

"Me too," said Jack.

Mum looked at him quickly, sharply. He could feel her watching him as he helped her fasten the baby sling. But he did not look at her.

As they wandered into the main part of the

village, Jack began to wonder if it had all been some kind of trick. He felt a tingle of recognition; yet the village seemed curiously altered. It was like dreams, where the house he was in had been his own house, yet different. But then, almost as the thought came, he saw a row of cottages ahead of him. The roofs were slate now, instead of thatch. Other than that, the house of Widow Cooper was almost unchanged. He ran towards it.

There was a plaque on the wall. Jack craned forward, eagerly.

> The first victim of the plague died here. George Viccars, a travelling tailor, lodged in this cottage with Mrs Cooper, a miner's widow, and her two sons. He died September the seventh, 1665. Edward Cooper, the second victim, died here September the twenty-second, 1665. Jonathan Cooper, also a victim, died here October second, 1665.

Jonathan! Jonathan had died too! Poor Widow Cooper. Both of her sons; dead within a few weeks of each other.

He remembered coming here in the rain, just after George Viccars' death. He remembered the widow's face peering out of the window. He remembered Parson Mompesson staring at him, as if he could see into his soul. All of those things had happened in this very place, behind the walls of this very cottage.

His mother ambled towards him, unable to keep up with him now that she had a baby to carry. She leaned over the low wall to read the wording on the plaque. Jack wondered what she would say if he told her that he had met them all, that he had been to Edward's funeral.

"I wonder who lives here now?" said Mum. "It must be a funny feeling, having people peering into your house. I don't think I'd like it very much."

"Come on! The church is just up here."

This was the part of Eyam he remembered best. He'd walked up this street during the wakes, when it had been filled with happy people enjoying the sunshine. It seemed grey now, in comparison.

And there was the church, almost exactly as it had been in 1665. He cast his mind back to Edward Cooper's funeral, and how he'd thought it was the funeral of George Viccars. It had been a shock when he'd found out. He thought of his excursion with Susannah in the dead of night, and how scared he'd been.

He imagined himself telling Mum. What would she say, now that there was no fever to account for his words? He'd noticed her watching him, as if looking for his reaction to everything they came across. His reaction? Or his recognition? What was she thinking?

He ran down the tarmac path to the back of the church, to the grave of Susannah's brothers. But search as he might, he could not find it.

It had been just here, hadn't it? Surely? He felt a twist of anxiety. But no, it hadn't. He glanced to his right and saw that he had not come quite far enough. The little headstone slanted now and he could make out only a few of the letters on it. But it was the same stone, the Roe stone.

Susannah had thought it was really something to have this headstone. He shook his head at the memory. "I can't read it any more." He ran his fingers over the faded lettering and saw Susannah again, holding the little earthenware vase filled with blue flowers.

"It's very old, Jack." Mum knelt beside him. "The weather wears things away, especially in exposed places like this."

Inside the church there was a lot of information about the plague. Jack wanted to explain the feeling it gave him, knowing that he'd been there when it happened; knowing that some of the people were his friends.

Mum was beckoning to him from the other side of the aisle.

"Look, Jack. It's the plague register, the

record of all the people who died in the plague."

He'd never read anything so fast in all his life. His eyes flew over the names: George Viccars, Edward Cooper, Peter Halksworth, Thomas Thorpe; on and on, name after name, whole families wiped out until finally: November the first, sixteen sixty-six, Abraham Morten.

There was no mention of Susannah or William or Mr and Mrs Roe. Did that mean they survived. Or . . .? He could not say it. Could not even think it. He looked at his mother who looked back at him thoughtfully. It was almost as if she knew what he was thinking.

"Dad told me," she said.

"Did he?" Jack felt a flicker of relief.

He so wanted someone to share this with. It was all too much for one person.

"What did he say?"

"He said you kept talking about someone called Susannah. That sometimes you seemed to think she was actually there."

Mum looked as if she was waiting for him to deny it.

He said, "What did Dad think about that?"

"He thought it was the fever; that you were delirious."

"Well, it wasn't." Jack hardly dared look at

his mother. He felt his face begin to redden. But it was now or never. If he missed this chance he would never be able to tell anyone the real story. It would start to fade from his mind like a forgotten dream.

"I need to know what happened to them," he said quietly.

Mum took some time to answer.

"I suppose we could try to find out if there are any more records," she said.

Jack turned to her; looked straight into her eyes. "I did meet them, you know."

"I know," she said. And smiled.

"Yes, the parish registers carry on after the plague," the man said.

"Could we see them?" Jack forgot his shyness and blurted the words out.

"Jack!" She didn't say, don't be cheeky, but that's what she meant. And it was her idea, not his!

"Well now, is it important?" the man asked.

Mum explained.

"Well, lots of schools do projects on Eyam. The registers would fall to bits if we let everyone look at them."

Yes, thought Jack, lots of schools do projects on Eyam. But I've never done one. I came here three hundred and twenty-seven years ago precisely, to see for myself. And now all my friends are dead.

"We've come an awfully long way," said Mum.

The man looked at them. "All right, then," he said. "As you're with your Mum, we'll see what we can do." He winked at Jack. "She's looking a bit tired and all. Keeping you awake nights, is he?"

"Yes." Mum smiled. The baby squawked obligingly.

At least it's got some uses, thought Jack, looking at his brother.

The writing was illegible in some parts and difficult to read in others. They bent their heads over the old books and searched the pages meticulously. Jack's neck ached and he hadn't found anything yet.

"Here!" Mum's voice made him jump.

"What?"

"Hannah Roe. Buried June the thirteenth, sixteen hundred and eighty-eight."

"That's it! That's it! That's the mother. The mother!"

Mum laughed as Jack almost danced in his chair. "Keep still or you'll knock the book off the table. Then we'll never find the others."

But they did.

Joshua Roe, buried January the ninth, sixteen hundred and ninety-two.

Susannah Roe, buried March the thirty-first, 1680.

Susannah, buried? Susannah, dead? He could almost hear her, mocking him in that superior way of hers. *Of course I am dead, boy. What else?* He saw her in the kitchen, rocking the cradle. He saw her walking down the lane and laughing at him. He saw her as he had seen her the very first time, sobbing and afraid. How could she be dead? How could she?

But she was, of course. And she hadn't been very old. Jack looked at the register again: buried March the thirty-first, 1680.

"She must have been about twelve or thirteen in 1665," he told Mum. "That would make her," he did some rapid calculations, "Twenty-seven or so. Only twenty-seven." Poor Susannah. She'd survived the plague, but she hadn't lived very long.

"She didn't marry either, by the looks of it. Or she'd have changed her name." Mum stroked the baby's hair. She had a faraway look on her face.

"Poor Susannah." He said it aloud this time.

"Yes, poor Susannah." Mum sighed. "But it wasn't unusual to die young in those days."

Didn't he know that better than anyone? Hadn't he seen her brothers' grave?

"You just have to think, Jack, that even if she'd lived to be a hundred, she'd still be dead by now."

"That's not the point, Mum."

"I suppose not."

And then he almost saw her, almost heard her voice. But it was a memory, nothing more. A memory of a muddy lane in Eyam, and raindrops in the hedges. Death is not an ending, boy, she had said. It is a new beginning. She would know by now if she'd been right. Or not.

They went back to the book. They had found everyone now, except William. They carried on searching. Jack's eyes danced with the strain of trying to decipher the cramped writing. They seemed to have been there for hours and were about to give up when Mum turned and plonked the baby in Jack's arms.

"I'll be quicker by myself. I'm a doctor. I'm used to bad handwriting."

It took another ten minutes.

"William Roe!" She almost shouted it. "Buried July the first, 1740." No wonder it had taken so long to find.

"He was an old man!" Jack counted again. "He must have been seventy-six when he died. Seventy-six!"

He remembered the baby sleeping in his cradle, and smiled to himself. What sort of a man had he been? Did the happy baby turn into a happy man? Jack would never know.

And now another baby slept in William's cradle.

"Little William with the fat legs and cheeky smile; an old man." Jack stretched forward and closed the book. It had all been worth it.

"William," said Mum. "That's a good name."

Jack looked down and smiled at his brother's round, grey eyes, searching out his own. He felt a tiny finger curl into his palm. William Rutherford. It was a good name. A very good name indeed.

Afterword

Eyam is a small village in the Derbyshire Peak District. It is a real place: a place you can visit. In 1665 plague came to Eyam; carried up from London in a box of cloth, it is said.

The story of the Eyam plague is a true story: it is the story of a village which sacrificed itself in order that the plague should not spread further. For the villagers, led by The Reverend William Mompesson, decided that no one should enter or leave the village until the plague was at an end.

The Earl of Devonshire arranged that food should be left at the edge of the village so that the people of Eyam should not starve in their isolation. The villagers paid for the food with money soaked in vinegar, to act as a disinfectant. This too, was left at the edge of the village, to avoid direct contact with anyone from the outside world.

These actions succeeded in stopping the plague from spreading, but the cost to the village was the loss of at least two hundred and fifty-nine lives.

In Eyam today, there are people living in houses which have been in their families for over three hundred years; perhaps the very same houses where their ancestors died of the plague.

At the moment there is a lot of research being carried out and a lot of new information being discovered. The people of Eyam are preparing to build a museum as a centre for this information, and to house the many plague relics which they possess.

If you should visit Eyam, you will find the village not so very different from how it must have been at the time of the plague. You will see the cottage of Widow Cooper, the church that Jack and Susannah visited at midnight, and the tomb of Catherine Mompesson, the vicar's wife, who died of the plague. Perhaps you will imagine a girl in a long brown dress and white bonnet: will see a resemblance to William in the little boy who walks by her side.

Perhaps, if you stretch out your mind across the years, they will seem quite close to you.

Linda Kempton